Dear Romance Reader,

Welcome to a world of breathtaking passion and never-ending romance.
Welcome to *Precious Gem Romances.*

It is our pleasure to present *Precious Gem Romances,* a wonderful new line of romance books by some of America's best-loved authors. Let these thrilling historical and contemporary romances sweep you away to far-off times and places in stories that will dazzle your senses and melt your heart.

Sparkling with joy, laughter, and love, each *Precious Gem Romance* glows with all the passion and excitement you expect from the very best in romance. Offered at a great affordable price, these books are an irresistible value—and an essential addition to your romance collection. Tender love stories you will want to read again and again, *Precious Gem Romances* are books you will treasure forever.

Look for eight fabulous new *Precious Gem Romances* each month—available only at Wal★Mart.

Lynn Brown, Publisher

# *LOVE IS THE ANSWER*

## *Abby Gray*

Zebra Books
Kensington Publishing Corp.

http://www.zebrabooks.com

ZEBRA BOOKS are published by

Kensington Publishing Corp.
850 Third Avenue
New York, NY 10022

Zebra and the Z logo Reg. U.S. Pat. & TM Off.

First Printing: December, 1997
10  9  8  7  6  5  4  3  2  1

Printed in the United States of America

# Chapter One

"Hellfire and damnation." Cassie frowned at her reflection in the cracked mirror above the lavatory in the women's rest room. "I need a scarf or a hat," she muttered, dragging a comb through the tangled red curls framing her small oval face. "I should just put a sign around my neck that says *Return Me To Cecil Gorman*." She forced all her wayward locks into a ponytail, wrapped a rubber band around it twice, and checked her watch.

She had only a few minutes until the passengers started reboarding the bus. Just one more hour and she'd be across the Texas state line and into Oklahoma. She desperately hoped Cecil wouldn't come looking for her. If the authorities said she had to go back to Cecil's farm in San Antonio, they had better get ready to put her body in a pine box, because she would never go back, not if she was still breathing.

She sighed deeply and walked out of the rest room, right in view of two uniformed policemen. Her heart skipped two beats, fluttered a couple of times, then began to race. A fine sweat formed on her upper lip as one policeman nudged the other one and nodded in her direction. No doubt about it . . . they had spotted her.

Cassie imagined the steely chilliness of the handcuffs they would clamp around her wrists. She scanned the diner connected to the bus stop, but the exit door was on the other side of the policemen, who continued to look her up and down suspiciously as they walked toward her.

She considered dashing back into the restroom, and crawling out a window into the bus yard, but the only window she had seen was too high for her to reach. Her mind raced from one part of the restroom to another, trying to remember anything she could use to reach it— a stool, a trash can, the sink, even the side of the stall— but nothing came to mind.

Cassie prayed for a way out. Then she saw him.

A young man sat alone at a table for two. He looked up from the menu he had been studying and directly at her. She smiled cheerily and waved when she caught his eye. Pretending she didn't know there were two policemen between her and freedom, she commanded her jelly-filled knees to carry her across the room.

Who was she? Ted wondered. When he'd glanced up, she'd acted as if she knew him. Maybe she was a waitress he'd met the last time he ate in this diner. She was undeniably pretty, even though she looked tired and a little scared. Whoever she was, she was going to be embarrassed when she found out he didn't have the first idea who she was or where he'd seen her before.

"Hi, honey," she said, loudly enough for the two policemen behind her to hear. She leaned down and brushed a light kiss across his cheek. "Please help me," she whispered in his ear. "Please say I'm with you." She slid into the chair across from him, and laid her left hand on his right one. Her green eyes looked desperate, even though a loving smile was plastered on her face.

Maybe the girl was deranged, Ted thought. Maybe this was one of those television shows where they videotaped practical jokes on unsuspecting people. All he wanted to do was eat his lunch, get in his trusty old truck, and go home to Oklahoma. He wasn't the right person for anyone to be playing a joke on, most assuredly not if it was going to be on national television.

"Excuse me," the older policeman drawled. Ted hadn't even noticed them behind the girl. "I'm Sheriff Bud Tucker and this is my deputy, Buzz Stevens. Who are you, gal?" he asked the girl.

"Why do you want to know?" Ted asked. The girl looked so nervous, she had to be in some kind of trouble. He didn't know what it was, but she looked so vulnerable, he couldn't believe she'd done anything really bad.

"Well, we were told to be on the lookout for a runaway from San Antonio. Seventeen-year-old girl, not too tall, with red hair." The sheriff looked closely at Cassie, who certainly fit that description.

Ted knew suddenly that this was no joke, because this innocent-looking young lady had a death grip on his hand. He shook his head. "Sorry. This is my girlfriend. We drove down here from Maysville, Oklahoma, just a little while ago." He paused. "And we're going to elope today," he added in a flash of inspiration that he hoped would inspire the officers to leave them alone. "My name is Ted Wellman and this is—" He looked at the petite redhead beside him trying to think of a name that fit her. "Well, we all call her Sassy."

The sheriff relaxed and chuckled. "You must be Bob Wellman's son. He's some poker player. Last time he was in town to pick up parts I lost a hundred dollars to him. I still haven't paid him back." He hitched his thumbs in his gun belt and swayed back and forth on his big feet. "Tell you what. My brother is the Justice of the Peace here. I'll just lead the way in my cruiser and you two kids can get married in his office, free of charge. And while you're getting hitched, I'll get you a room at the Yucca Inn for the night. My sister runs the place. When you get home you tell your dad that Bud Tucker has paid up that hundred dollars and is ready for another poker game when he gets back down here."

Cassie squeezed Ted's hand even harder. He got the messages traveling frantically down from her mind through her fingers. Ted knew if he hesitated the game was over. The sheriff would win. The girl would lose, and they would put him so far away for aiding and abetting a minor run-away they'd have to pump sunshine and oxygen into his cell.

"Well, this *is* our lucky day." Ted grinned from ear to ear and patted the girl's hand. "The sheriff owes my dad money and we get a free honeymoon. Can't beat a deal like that. Lead the way, gentlemen." He pulled the girl up to stand beside him and casually draped his arm around her shoulders. "Didn't I tell you it would all work out, sweetheart?" he said, steering her to his battered pickup and opening the door for her.

"Oh, damn," she exploded when they were safely inside. "What are we going to do now? I can't marry you. I don't even know you."

"Settle down," Ted said calmly. "If they don't go in the Justice's office, we'll just tell the man we changed our minds and walk out. By the way, I really am Ted Wellman and my dad is Bob Wellman. Who are you?"

"My name is Cassie Stewart. You came pretty close," she told him.

"I figured I'd just tell him that was your nickname, whatever your real name was."

"Oh."

She looked out of the corner of her eye at the man sitting beside her. She'd never seen anyone so handsome. His hair was blacker than a raven's wing, and his pecan-colored eyes were flecked with gold. He stood more than six feet, towering above her five feet, two inches, even when they were sitting beside each other in the truck. He looked like he'd probably played football in high school and maybe college, and if he ever crossed the California border, Hollywood would be waiting for him with open arms and a million-dollar contract.

"Well, I'm not marrying you," she declared, more for her own benefit than his. "You could be a criminal. Or already married."

He shook his head. "Nope. I'm just a farmer from southern Oklahoma. And I'm single. But you *are* going to marry me, at least temporarily. You're underage and you're a runaway, according to that sheriff. I'd rather marry you—just for today, of course—than go to jail for you."

Ted was only half-joking. He looked over and saw that Cassie was almost in tears, and felt a wave of sympathy for her, which surprised him. He hadn't felt much emotion—not love, hate, tears, joy, anger, or pain—in more than seven years.

"Running away isn't a crime," she said through clenched teeth. "Not from that Cecil, who says I stole from him. I didn't. And I will not marry you." Two spots of bright red colored her cheeks and her green eyes danced, daring him to argue with her.

"You don't have a choice, Cassie. It's me or—what was his name? Cecil."

The black and white cruiser ahead of them stopped in front of a small white building. A rusty pole supported a squeaky sign, which needed a paint job as badly as the house did. The writing on the sign promised certified copies, notary public available, and weddings in fifteen minutes, all from Samuel T. Tucker, Justice of the Peace.

Bud and Buzz waved at them to get out of the pickup. "Come right in, kids. Hey, I forgot to ask you. You got a blood test, didn't you?"

Cassie took a deep breath. "No, we didn't have time," she lied.

"Damn," the sheriff muttered. "Well, I can get you married and I can get you a room, but the blood test the hospital does will cost another hundred dollars if you want the results right away. I don't owe Bob Wellman that much money. You got another hundred dollars, boy?"

" 'Course I do," Ted said. "I told you we came here to get married. I was just hoping you could use your influence and we could skip the blood test. Temporarily, anyway."

The sheriff rubbed his chin with his hand. "Nope. Can't do it, boy. Got lots of influence, but it wouldn't be legal and proper without that test. Just leave your truck parked right there and we'll run over to the hospital in my cruiser. We can stop by the courthouse on the way and pick up a marriage license too. I almost forgot about that."

"Fine with me." Ted grabbed Cassie's hand and pulled her into the backseat of the cruiser with him. "Sure is nice of you to help us out, Sheriff."

Cassie could've strangled him with one hand tied behind her back. He was digging the hole that they were tumbling into deeper and deeper. How was she ever going to get out of this? She noted the landmarks of the little town they were driving through in case she had to run away again.

Bud Tucker stopped the black and white at the emergency room entrance of the hospital. He unbuckled his seat belt and opened the door. "Well, let's go in and get the blood test over with. You don't faint at the sight of blood, do you, gal?" Bud studied Cassie, who was almost trembling.

"No, sir," she said.

"Good," he nodded. "I know the doctor and all the nurses here. I'll get them to rush you through and we'll be back at Sam's place in a few minutes. You be sure and tell old Bob Wellman that I helped you a lot," he said to Ted.

"Yes, sir. I sure will," Ted agreed.

True to his word, Bud Tucker's influence got them the blood tests and the marriage license in record time. The sheriff stood right beside the nurse when she drew blood, and then he peered over the kids' shoulders when they produced driver's licenses to prove that they were indeed Ted Wellman and Cassie O'Malley. He had a sneaking suspicion that the girl's name was really Cassandra Stewart, but then she flipped open her billfold to show her license. It clearly said Cassandra O'Malley. Had Ted said her name was Cassie when he'd introduced the girl to them? Sheriff Bud Tucker sighed. His hearing must be getting as bad as his wife kept telling him. He was almost positive Ted had called her Sassy.

"Tell Sam I said not to charge you a dime," the sheriff said when he pulled the cruiser into the Justice's driveway again. "Me and Buzz will rent you a room at the Yucca Inn while you're getting married."

Cassie's brain went numb for the second time in only an hour. What could Ted be thinking of? He could turn around at any second and tell the law officers he didn't know who she was, and walk away from it all. What would she do if they really did say the wedding vows and then he expected her to be really married to him in every sense of the word?

Samuel Tucker was a short, fat man with bulldog jowls that hung down on either side of his mushy lips. His slick, round head was as bald as a pumpkin, and it didn't look like it had ever sprouted a hair through the years. It was easy to see that he and Bud were brothers. They both sported guts resembling over-inflated tractor tires hanging out over their big, silver belt buckles.

"Wedding license looks all right. But I gotta see some other ID," Samuel said. "That's the law."

Ted dug in his pocket for his wallet again.

"Theodore Ashton Wellman, age 21," Samuel said aloud as he looked at the driver's license.

"How 'bout you, miss?" Samuel asked Cassie.

She pulled out her billfold and showed him her driver's license.

"Cassandra Elizabeth Rose O'Malley. Whew!" Sam chuckled. "That's a long name for such a short girl. Let's

see now, your age. Says here on the license you're eighteen.
Guess they goofed, didn't they?"

Without a word, Ted took a fifty-dollar bill from his
wallet and laid it on top of the marriage license form. *Just
get this farce over with,* he thought. *Uncle Ash can undo it
tomorrow, even if he isn't the world's greatest lawyer. Then this
piece of redhaired trouble from hell's back door can be on her merry
way. Good Lord, all I wanted to do was have some pie and coffe
and go home and here I am about to get married to a total stranger.*

"Tryin' to bribe me, son?" Sam picked up the bill with
alacrity and put it in his shirt pocket. "Folks at the courthouse didn't notice that she's only seventeen, did they?
Well, I guess I didn't see it either. Now . . . where was I?"

The full impact of what he was about to do slammed
into Ted. His chest ached, his mouth felt like it was filled
with cotton, and there was an army of butterflies going
crazy in his stomach. Ladies had jitters like this, not full-
grown, twenty-one-year-old men.

But it wasn't as if it was the end of the world, he reminded
himself. Or even a real marriage. Uncle Ash would wave
a magic law book and take care of it all as soon as he got
home.

Sam commenced the ceremony, speaking rapidly.

"Do you, Theodore Ashton Wellman, Take Cassandra
Elizabeth Rose O'Malley to be your lawful wedded wife,
for better or for worse, in sickness or health . . ." Sam
droned on and on. No one was really listening. Even the
witness, who'd shuffled in from the park bench outside to
earn the five dollars that Samuel usually slipped him for
these occasions, seemed to be on the verge of slumber.

"Well, do you?" Sam asked loudly.

Ted snapped to.

"I do," he said, crossing his fingers behind his back. It
was a childish gesture, he knew, but he did it anyway.

"Do you, Cassandra . . ." Sam wondered for a second if
he'd get a reply out of this girl. He'd performed hundreds
of weddings through the years and he'd seen dozens of

girls with nervous jitters, but he'd never seen a bride as scared and this one. She looked like she might bolt and run like a jackrabbit.

Cassie wanted to cry.

She had always imagined her wedding day, envisioned herself in a church, standing beside a man who'd swept her off her feet, who had promised to give her the sun, the moon, and all the stars. She was supposed to be wearing a white satin gown and a veil of sheerest illusion, not a faded red sweatshirt, ancient sneakers and bleached-out jeans. One tiny tear finally found its way up from the bottom of her soul, hung on her thick eyelashes, and spilled down her cheek. She wiped it away with the back of her hand.

"Do you?" Sam asked again. She hadn't heard the rest of the vow.

"I do," she whispered.

"Well, well, well." The sheriff and the deputy opened the side door to the J.P.'s office. "Looks like we got here just in time for the ceremony. You can kiss the bride," he said joshingly. "You're married now."

Ted looked down into Cassie's green eyes. He drew her close to him, tipped her chin back with his hand, and hoped for the best. He put his lips on hers and kissed her hard enough to convince that fool sheriff. Wonder of wonders, Cassie kissed him back.

He felt an indescribable electricity course through him, and he wished he knew why. This girl meant nothing to him . . .

"Okay. She can consider herself kissed," Sheriff Tucker said hastily. "Buzz, let's get these newlyweds over to the Yucca Inn and have my sister show them their honeymoon suite. Your room's right next to the ice machine so it's real convenient if you want to chill some of them wine coolers to celebrate."

Cassie wondered if the sheriff had yet another relative who owned the local liquor store, but decided not to ask.

* * *

She was speechless with anger, mostly at herself. She crossed her arms, huffed, and stomped the floor of the pickup as Ted drove behind the all-too-familiar cruiser. Tears made rivers down her cheeks, and she felt like she'd just swallowed a stick of dynamite with a short fuse.

Ted grinned when he thought about their kiss. It had been the high point of this crazy day, that was for sure. He stole a glance at Cassie just in time to see the tears break over their long-lashed dams and spill down her fair cheeks. She put her hands over her eyes and sobbed.

"Hey." Ted patted her arm. "Don't cry. Come on now. Hush. My uncle is a lawyer and he'll undo this as soon as we get to Maysville. He can file an annulment or an uncontested divorce for us. Please don't cry. Besides, what will Bud and Buzz say if you're in tears when we get to our little love nest?"

"You shut up!" Cassie pointed an accusing finger at him. "Don't you dare tease me. I'm sorry I ever saw you. Or talked you into this lunatic scheme." She sobbed even harder.

"I seem to remember that I talked you into it," Ted replied calmly.

"Oh, you did—but you said you didn't want to—I'm underage—" Cassie's emotional state made her altogether incoherent. She struggled for self-control as Ted handed her a clean bandanna handkerchief.

"Blow your nose. Calm down," he said patiently. He pulled up in front of the Yucca Inn. "Listen to me, Cassie. It really would be best if you weren't throwing a hissy fit when we get out of this pickup. You don't want good ole Bud and Buzz to start asking a million questions, now do you? Then we'll both be in trouble, as well as married." He grabbed a suitcase from behind the seat and helped Cassie out of the truck. She made a determined effort to smile at the waiting officers, but it came out more like a grimace.

Buzz and Bud led the way. "Here it is. Lover's paradise," Buzz said proudly. He swung the door open with a flourish, and tossed the key on the bed. He elbowed the sheriff, who was smiling like a possum eating grapes through a barbed wire fence. "Paid for, too. Don't forget to tell your dad that him and the sheriff is squared up, now."

Ted had spent Tuesday and Wednesday at the De-Luxe Motel on the other side of town. The comparison between that place and this was like the difference between sunshine and absolute darkness. He set his suitcase down with a heavy thud, and locked the door behind the two officers when they left.

He surveyed the bed, which looked as if it had been dragged by a team of wild oxen over the Texas rangeland during the days of Daniel Boone and the Alamo. There was no doubt that Methuselah's mother had rocked him to sleep in the splintery rocking chair sitting in the corner. The carpet had to be a reject from someone's old outhouse, and if there weren't fleas under the sheets Ted would eat his Stetson, and have his worn-out Roper boots for dessert. "What a dump. Sorry, Cassie. Listen, I can sleep in the rocker, and you can have the bed," he offered. "Or maybe we can just sneak out when Bud and Buzz go home for the night."

"Oh, shut up!" Cassie glared at him again, just as she had in the pickup. "Who cares?" She threw herself down on the bed and curled up in a ball.

"Now what did I do?" he asked in exasperation. "I said we could get this marriage undone tomorrow. I kept those two characters from sending you back to wherever it is you're running from. What reason do you have to be mad at me?"

She sat up and wiped away still more tears with the bottom of her sweatshirt. "Ted, I am an O'Malley," she said, expecting him to understand. He didn't. She had said her name as if all the confusion would disappear if only he would understand how important it was that she was an O'Malley and she'd just remembered it. So what? Ted thought angrily. He didn't give a royal damn if she was related to the Queen of England by this point.

"You *were* an O'Malley. So? Now you're legally a Wellman and tomorrow you can be an O'Malley again. So what?" He threw the suitcase on the arms of the rocking chair and opened it.

"Bud and Buzz were looking for Cassandra Stewart," she tried to explain. "My mother's maiden name was Stewart and when she died I went to live with my Granny Stewart, so everyone just called me Cassie Stewart. I even went to school under that name. Don't you see? If I had been able to think straight, I could've just shown them my driver's license which says I'm an O'Malley."

"Cassie, you had that driver's license out in the hospital—" Ted stopped and fumed. It was too late now to scold her.

"I was scared stiff," she pleaded. "The sheriff was looking over my shoulder when I pulled out the license and I didn't even look at it. I didn't know what I was doing, anymore than you did. But I'm sorry. If I had half a brain, I wouldn't be married to you and I'd be on that bus to Oklahoma City."

She pounded the threadbare pillow with her fist, and a small tornado of feathers burst upward. Cassie choked, and brushed them off her face and clothes.

Ted took a clean T-shirt out of his suitcase.

"Look, why don't you take a nice, warm shower, if this dump has hot water, and put this on. Once I get home, Uncle Ash will start annulment proceedings and I'll get you to Oklahoma City somehow. Relax, will you?"

"Oh, sure. This has to be the most relaxing situation I have ever been in."

She snatched the T-shirt out of his hand, started toward the bathroom, and suddenly dropped into a heap on the floor. Ted gathered her up in his arms, afraid for a second that she'd died, but he was reassured to feel her heartbeat against his chest. "Cassie, wake up. Open your eyes, girl. What do I do now?"

"I feel so dizzy . . ." she mumbled. "I'm—hungry."

Ted laid her gently down on the bed and looked at her carefully. She was on the thin side, and she did look pale. "How long has it been since you've eaten?"

"Can't remember," she said weakly. She didn't open her eyes. "Is this Thursday? Didn't get to eat yesterday because Cecil was mad. Tuesday, maybe Monday. I had some milk Tuesday, I think."

"Listen to me." He bent over her. "I'm going to buy food and bring it back. Don't try to stand up. Promise? You might get dizzy and faint again."

She nodded but her eyes stayed closed.

Questions plagued Ted as he drove to a fried chicken place only a block away. She hadn't eaten for two or three days because Cecil was mad. Who was Cecil anyway? Was she running from an abusive husband? Maybe that's why she'd been so dead set against marrying him, even as a ruse to evade the sheriff.

Unfortunately, that very same sheriff and the deputy were sitting in the first booth, with Sam, when Ted walked into the fried chicken place.

"You kids worked up an appetite already?" Buzz winked and laughed. "Must be great to be young."

"Yeah." Ted winked back at them and quickly gave the girl at the register his order. He wanted to get out of there and back to Cassie, fast.

"Don't forget to remember us to your daddy," Sam hollered as Ted left with a red-and-white cardboard box of chicken and biscuits.

"Sure will. Thanks for all you did for me and my—uh—wife." Ted almost tripped over the word.

Cassie lay rolled up in a ball, fast asleep. But the savory smell of chicken drifted through her subconscious. Deep

in her dream, she'd thrown her schoolbooks on the rumps-
prung sofa just inside the front door, and her granny was
dishing up supper in the kitchen. "Let's eat. You can study
later," her granny told her as she poured gravy into the
cracked bowl with the blue cornflowers on the side . . .

The dream began to fade and Cassie couldn't will it to
remain. But when she opened her eyes, the chicken smell
was still very real. It came from the cheery red-and-white
box that Ted was holding. He took out a biscuit.

"Nibble on this," Ted said gently. "You might get sick
if you eat too fast."

She ignored his advice and wolfed the biscuit, and a
piece of white meat. "I'd be embarrassed to eat like this
if I wasn't half-starved," she said between ravenous bites.
"Ted, I'm really sorry about this. Are you sure your uncle
can undo what we've done tomorrow? Lord, I don't want
to be married." She rambled on as she kept eating, but
Ted couldn't quite make out everything she was saying.
Probably better to let her eat her fill, and then she'd be
able to think straight.

"I've got to go make a phone call," Ted said. "You just
keep eating 'til you're full. There's a piece of apple pie
somewhere in the bottom of the box."

"Lock the door and take the key with you. I'll have a
shower when I get finished because I'm going to need one.
If you don't mind, I will borrow that T-shirt you offered."
She smiled at him for the first time, and he smiled back.

Ted found a pay phone in front of the office and dialed
*0* and a familiar number, and told the operator to make
the call collect. He waited, keeping an eye on room number
thirteen. From now on, that would be his unlucky number.
But then, he wouldn't be there ever again. In a few weeks,
it wouldn't matter what room he'd spent the first hours
of married life in. In a few years, this would be just a funny
story to tell his children, when he had some.

"Uncle Ash, this is Ted," he said, when he heard the
voice at the other end of the line accept the call.

"You're late for supper," Ash said. "Did you have trouble with that old truck? I've told you not to depend on that rattletrap, especially when you go out of state."

"The truck is fine," Ted said. "Listen, I had planned on leaving right after lunch when the parts Dad sent me for came in. But something came up." He paused and scratched his head, trying to figure out just how in hell he was going to explain what had come up. "I'm in a jam. Maybe you and I can talk about it over breakfast tomorrow morning. I'm staying here tonight but I'll be home early."

"I'll save you a couple of strips of bacon then," Ash joked. "So what kind of a jam are you in?"

Ted took a deep breath.

"I got married. And I need you to unmarry me, pronto," he said.

Ash let out a husky chuckle, which became a laugh, and finally a full-fledged roar.

"See you at breakfast, nephew. I'll be there. I wouldn't miss the fireworks for all the tea in China and half the dirt in Texas!"

# Chapter Two

After devouring enough fried chicken to feed a harvest crew and following Ted's advice to relax with a warm shower, Cassie put on his T-shirt. It fell to her knees. She crawled into bed, determined not to shut her eyes until Ted was back from making his phone call and fast asleep on the floor, or in the rocking chair, or wherever. He seemed like a decent sort, but she wasn't about to put her trust in him or any other man. Her experiences with the loathsome Cecil had taught her everything she didn't want to know about men.

But Cassie was curled up in a ball and asleep again, when Ted returned. He sat down in the rocker, and thought about the day while he took off his boots. It just didn't seem real.

However, the redheaded girl sleeping under the ratty bedspread certainly was. He suddenly remembered the arousing kiss she'd bestowed on him in the Justice of the Peace's office.

He studied her lovely face, troubled even in her sleep, and shook his head. She seemed so vulnerable—and so innocent—that his heart went out to her. He told himself silently not to look at her anymore.

Ted didn't even realize he'd fallen asleep sitting up in the rocker until Cassie shook him awake just about four o'clock. "Let's get going before the sheriff and Deputy Dawg wake up," she whispered.

He cracked open one eyelid. The room was still dark and he could barely see her standing over him. She was wearing some baggy garment that looked vaguely familiar . . . his T-shirt, he realized. it pleased him to see her in it.

Ted's neck was sore and his arm tingled. "Ouch," he muttered. "Give me time to take a shower and brush my teeth. I'm not even awake."

They didn't talk any more from the time they got into the truck until they saw the Texas state line in their rearview mirror. Ted sighed with relief when they crossed it into Oklahoma, glad down to the soles of his boots to be out of Bud Tucker's jurisdiction.

"We'll be at my folks' farm by breakfast," he told Cassie. "Want to tell me why you were on the run before we get there?"

"No. Not particularly. But I appreciate your help, honest I do. We're out of state now, so why don't you just pull over and let me out? I can hitch a ride to Oklahoma City from here," she said firmly.

"Damn it all to hell and back!" Ted slapped the steering wheel with both his hands, amazing himself with his sudden outburst of anger. Whether it was the lack of sleep or the unexpected feelings of protectiveness this girl seemed to inspire in him, he couldn't say, but something was making him mad. "Didn't your momma ever tell you what happens to girls who hitch rides? Don't you know better than to get in a car with a complete stranger?" His voice got louder with every word.

"Don't you dare shout at me!" she yelled right back, startled beyond belief. This man had been pretty quiet until this minute. *"You're* almost a complete stranger, even if that sheriff does know your daddy. Besides, my momma died the day I was born, but my granny always told me not to get in a stranger's car. She didn't think to tell me not to marry a complete stranger. We both thought I had better sense than that!" Cassie jerked her head around to stare out the window.

She *had* planned to tell him the reason why, especially since he'd been so nice about everything. But he didn't have to yell at her like that. What did he care if she hitch-hiked or not? In her admittedly limited experience, men only cared about women when they wanted something from them. But this man seemed different. He'd been genuinely kind—and he'd kept his hands off her, even when she'd been sleeping.

"If you want to know why I ran away—well, there's not that much to tell," Cassie said finally. "Hell, I might as well tell my whole life story. It's a long way to Oklahoma. Want the Reader's Digest condensed version?"

"Okay," Ted said cautiously. He was curious about her, and even if she made up everything as she went along, it would beat listening to the hellfire-and-brimstone preachers on the early morning radio.

*Here goes,* Cassie thought, and took a deep breath. She thought for a moment. *What difference does it make if he knows my life story? When the day is over, we'll never see each other again, anyway. He'll stay on his farm, wherever it is, and raise his pigs or whatever he raises, and someday he'll find a girl who'll be happy to marry a farmer, and I'll be on my own in Oklahoma City.*

"My mother died the day I was born. I told you that. Sorry. I'm repeating myself already." Cassie toyed with the worn strap of her purse. "She was Rose Stewart before she married my father, Patrick O'Malley. Granny Stewart told me I got my red hair from my father, but my green eyes were just like my mother's. My daddy died two months before I was born, in an oil well accident. So that's why my granny raised me.''

The affectionate tone of her voice told Ted that Cassie's grandmother had loved her very much—and that she had been a very important person in her granddaughter's young life. He wondered where the old woman was now, and whether she knew that Cassie was a runaway.

Cassie stopped, and stared out the window, noticing that the land had begun to roll gently in little hills. There were more trees and less flat land than she was used to, but it wasn't so very different from where she'd grown up.

"So you grandmother brought you up, huh? Sounds like she meant a lot to you," Ted encouraged her to continue.

Cassie just nodded. "My granny was everything to me." She paused. "She started teaching me my letters when I was three years old," she continued after a while. "It wasn't long before I was reading. She said I took to it like a duck to water. When she enrolled me in kindergarten, I was so far ahead of the other kids, they put me in the first grade. Then halfway through, they advanced me to the second grade. Granny was so proud. She said I'd be in college before she knew it."

Cassie stopped again, and wiped away a tear.

"Hey," Ted said softly. "I didn't mean you had to tell me everything—especially if it upsets you. We can just ride along quietly," he said. He had a hunch the rest of her life story might be too painful to tell.

"If you're going to understand today, you have to know about yesterday," she said in a dull voice. "I graduated from high school when I was barely sixteen. My granny talked to the principal and he talked to a college program administrator who let me start a medical secretary training course. I was interested in the health care field, and that seemed like a good place to start."

"Sure is. You know, I've got an uncle who's a doctor in Maysville," Ted said. He didn't add that his uncle might need a secretary. This girl didn't seem to like being helped too much, and it'd probably be best if he stopped trying to.

Cassie didn't even hear his comment about his uncle. "Anyway, I finished the first year and was enrolled for the second. When I left for the first day of school last fall, Granny was fine, waving goodbye to me from the porch, proud of me as ever. By the time I got home that day she was dead of a stroke."

Cassie shut her eyes and saw the frail old woman who had been both mother and father to her. The little lady who'd told her to take life like a bull . . . by the horns, look it straight in the eye and dare it to challenge her. Her grandmother's body had looked so small in the cheap casket. After the preacher had said the routine words for the benefit of the few relatives who'd cared enough to show up at the funeral, her granny had been buried. And that had been that.

"A neighbor said I could live with her and finish school, but it didn't work out. You see, Granny had another daughter when she was real young . . . my mother's half sister. It's kind of a tangled story, but my half aunt married a drunk and they had a son. Cecil. I suppose he's my half cousin or something like that."

She took a deep breath.

"I never did like him, but when Granny died, there he was, crawling out from whatever rock he'd lived under until then. Since he was the only living relative I had, the State Department of Child Welfare said I had to go live with him. Oh, he was willing, all right. But when we got to his farm . . ." Cassie trailed off.

Ted waited patiently, not knowing if the story had ended or if there was still more to come.

She sighed and started again in the same monotone.

"The first day we got to Cecil's farm, his wife told me

I'd already had too much schooling and it was time for me to earn my keep. That meant getting up at dawn to work in the garden, the fields, or the house, or wherever else they could think. Just so long as I was slaving sixteen hours a day. I don't mind hard work, but if either of them thought I hadn't done my chores right then I had to do without supper or breakfast, and sometimes I got no food at all for the whole day. Anyway, to make a long story a little shorter, Cecil tried to get me to unlock my bedroom door after midnight a couple of nights ago. He was whispering on the other side of the door, saying that if I'd just unlock it, he would let me eat breakfast the next morning. I could figure out what he was after. So I waited until he gave up and then I took my mother's wedding rings from my dresser, and just sneaked out. I walked six miles into San Antonio, hocked them, and used the money to buy a ticket to Oklahoma City. You know the rest." She ended her tale with a small sigh.

Ted's stomach felt empty but he wasn't hungry. He wondered if pity felt like this. Cassie hadn't been dealt a fair hand when life had shuffled the deck. No wonder she'd seemed so vulnerable—yet she had a stubborn streak that he admired, too. Cassie had endured too much for someone who was only seventeen . . . the thought jerked him back to the present. Her age alone had to be grounds for a speedy annulment—he was certain Uncle Ash would agree. Ted didn't want to cause this girl any more trouble than she'd already been through.

But he wasn't exactly sure he never wanted to see her again, either.

"So why are you going to Oklahoma City?" He cleared his throat, trying for an easy tone. "Any kinfolk there?"

"Nope." Cassie shook her head but wouldn't look at him. "Only relative I have in this world is Cecil Gorman and if I never see him again, it will be too soon. Oklahoma City was as far as I could get on the money from the wedding rings, that's all."

"Oh." Ted couldn't find another word in his vocabulary.

The Oklahoma sunrise seemed to welcome Ted and Cassie on that particular morning. The dark began to fade and the pale light showed the branches of trees, reaching out as if beckoning the two young people in the pickup truck home. A huge, brilliant red sun peeped over the eastern horizon, and Cassie turned to watch it rise, smiling a little.

She turned back to sneak a look at Ted, who very rarely smiled, she realized suddenly. Cassie sensed an unspoken sadness within him that she didn't dare ask about—after all, she probably would never see him again after this day. His somber expression seemed to match the seasonal bleakness of the landscape around them, and she wished suddenly that she could have a chance to know this thoughtful stranger better. But that would take time, and time was something they didn't have.

They passed a sign welcoming them to Maysville, and were soon driving down Main Street, which was only a few blocks long. The Christmas decorations were still up in the darkened shop windows, and a hand-lettered sign in one said *Closed Until After New Year's. Have A Happy And Don't Drink And Drive.*

Cassie realized that December was almost over, and Christmas had come and gone without her ever celebrating. Well, there hadn't been much to celebrate, come to think of it.

They quickly passed through the outskirts of town, and were now driving through farmland.

"Are you really a farmer?" she asked shyly. "This is pretty country around here."

"Sure am," he replied. "I have a few acres of my own right next to my dad's land." His dad, who was going to skin him alive for marrying this girl. His ever-loving uncles might even tack his hide to the smokehouse door to remind all future generations of Wellmans never to do anything so crazy again . . . but if they'd seen Cassie looking so lost and frightened, they might have taken a notion to rescue her themselves. "It's only two more miles. Momma will have breakfast ready by the time we get there. Daddy has always liked to eat early and my younger sister Alicia takes forever to get ready for school, so she has to get up early."

"What?" Cassie said, alarmed. "I didn't ask you to take me home—as if I were a stray puppy. I'll just get out right here. Ted Wellman, stop this truck and let me out, now! I'll jump out if you don't. I swear I will!"

Ted didn't react. His family would've expected that. Big, gentle Ted seldom got worked up enough to care about anything anymore.

But Cassie had no way of knowing that. She looked at his expressionless profile, and then kicked him hard, in his right shin. Ted didn't so much as flinch.

"Now, why did you go and do that? I'm not going to hurt you, girl. A good breakfast wouldn't kill you."

"Let me out!" she shrilled. "I don't want to meet your family and I don't care if we did just get married!"

Ted gritted his teeth. This little tornado was kinda getting to him. He cursed his own good nature. So he'd saved her from that dumb sheriff and now she was treating him like this. Well, she could damn well settle down and listen to reason. Even if he had to yell again.

"Listen, Cassie," he shouted. His vocal cords hadn't worked that hard for a very long time. "You said you used all your money to buy a ticket to Oklahoma City. Well, what are you going to do when you get there? You've got no money, no place to stay, and no prospects of a job. Use that brain your granny was so proud of, will you?"

He paused, and she looked at him like a scared rabbit.

"I'm going to turn this truck around at the next section line and if you so much as make a move to jump out, I'll— I'll—" He couldn't think of any reasonable threat so he pounded the steering wheel instead. "I told you Uncle Ash could get us out of this. But he can't do it quickly unless you stick around to sign the papers. You owe me that much, and that's all I'm asking.''

Tears spilled out under her thick eyelashes. She was so mad she couldn't utter a sound. For the second time that morning he was yelling at her as if she were a child. She wasn't going to stand for it, and . . . Ted pulled off the road suddenly, and Cassie clutched the edge of the bench seat to keep from slamming against him.

"Welcome home, Mrs. Wellman," Ted said sarcastically. He parked the truck beneath a huge pecan tree in the center of an oval driveway. Cassie just stared, shocked.

"Home?" she said softly.

She had expected a small frame house, the kind a dirt farmer in the heart of Texas might have. The kind with scaling paint and a dirt yard with a beat-up car jacked up on concrete blocks, and an old tractor peeking out from behind the house.

What stood before her eyes looked like a picture from one of those historical Western romance novels she liked to read sometimes. The farmhouse—if it could be called a mere farmhouse—was three stories high, with balconies, and a wraparound verandah. The landscaped yard was straight out of one of those gardening books her granny had pored every spring. There was enough house—and enough land around it—for several generations of a large, prosperous, happy family.

"There's Uncle Ash's pickup." Ted pointed to a brand-new black club-cab truck parked in the driveway. "And Uncle Brock must be here. Yup. That's his red Cadillac over there." He shook his head, dreading the confrontation that he was expecting with his family.

"Who are they?" Cassie asked, bewildered, her own anger chilled by more than the cold north wind whipping through the truck when Ted opened the door. "What do they all do for a living? Run a gold mine?"

"Uncle Ash is the lawyer who's going to unmarry us. Uncle Brock is Maysville's general practitioner. They're

my daddy's brothers. My daddy owns some oil wells and
he runs an oil well maintenance business, too. But he
started out as a farmer, the way I'm starting out.''

"Why are they all here? I think you missed somebody.
Who owns that white pickup truck?'' she asked nervously.

"Oh, that's mine. I only use this one for trips down to
Texas to pick up oil well parts. I don't want to scratch up
my nice new truck. But I guess you would've preferred to
be rescued in the new one.''

Ted guided Cassie up the stairs onto the front verandah
without another word from her.

"You ready to meet your new in-laws?'' he asked, in a
tone she didn't particularly like. "Dear,'' he added, in an
even more mocking tone.

Cassie shook her head no, and looked almost ready to
bolt. Ted got a firm grip on her elbow and almost pushed
her through the front door.

His father, Bob Wellman, greeted them warmly from
inside the living room. Ted was a little surprised. A warm
welcome was the last thing he'd expected. He looked over
at his Uncle Ash, who was sitting on the blue velvet sofa
with his wife Maggie cuddled up next to him. Uncle Brock
saw the two of them enter from his spot in the den, and
he set his newspaper down and came in, too.

Ted's younger sister Alicia was taking exquisite glass
ornaments from a huge Christmas tree, and packing them
carefully in an old wooden chest that looked hand-hewn.
Cassie figured that the pretty dark-haired girl was a little
older than she was—perhaps in college—and she looked
wistfully at the ornaments. She had always wanted a big,
old-fashioned, *real* tree like that every year, but she and
Granny had made do with a bitty one from the drugstore.

Ash had a definite twinkle in his eye, Ted noticed nervously. "Hello, nephew,'' the older man said in a booming
voice. "Is that the jam you were in?'' He nodded toward
Cassie.

Ted could've kicked his uncle, but instead he introduced

him and his sister to her. Cassie managed only a nearly inaudible hello.

A short woman came from what Cassie supposed was the kitchen. Long, dark hair, streaked just slightly with gray, was pulled back at the nape of her neck. She had the softest brown eyes Cassie had ever seen, and she was wearing a denim skirt and a red sweater, both covered with a bibbed apron with lace on the edges.

"Ted?" She raised an expressive eyebrow.

"Momma, I want you to meet Cassie," he said. "Cassie, this is my mother, Maria Wellman." There. That had to be the most awkward moment of his life, and it was over.

Cassie nodded. "Hello, everybody. Sorry to bother you. But I want all of you to know I appreciate what Ted did to help me out. Now if you'll just show me where to sign the papers, I'll be on my way." She tried to sound as if she got married and divorced all the time, and it wasn't any big deal.

"Sit down," Ted said to her. "Let me explain," he said to his folks.

"That might be nice, son," his father said, amiably enough.

Ted started at the beginning from when he'd looked up and seen Cassie for the first time barely twenty-four hours ago, and he didn't stop until he'd told it all, including that she'd fainted from hunger, and that she had threatened to jump out of his truck.

When he finally finished, Cassie felt ashamed to the bone. Everyone in the room knew she was dirt poor, had only the clothes on her back, had put their son in an awful fix, and had no idea of what to do next. She wished passionately that she could vanish from their lives in a puff of smoke, but Ted had made his point.

She owed it to him to stay, if only for a short while.

Maria watched the girl while Ted told his story. Then she watched her son. For the first time in many years, he'd shown some emotion. It was the first time he'd been angry,

the first time he'd cared about anyone or anything enough
to take a stand, since longer than she could remember. And
if her crazy son thought that for one minute his mother was
going to stand by and let the girl who'd somehow wrought
this miracle just walk out the door, he had taco filling for
brains.

A brilliant idea occurred to her.

"Brock," she said suddenly. "You need a medical secretary in the clinic. This girl needs a job. That's the first
thing we can help her with . . ." Maria gave him a meaningful look.

Brock gave Ash an equally meaningful look.

Ash didn't need to be told in words what his sister-in-
law was hinting at. After all, he was married to her sister
and the two women were closer than twins. So Maria didn't
think this scrawny girl should sign an annulment . . . she
seemed to want Cassie to stay. If that's what Maria wanted,
then he would move heaven and earth and sell shares in
hell to make that happen.

Ash exchanged a glance with Bob, who nodded almost
imperceptibly.

The family had agreed.

"I do need a medical secretary, Cassie," Brock said, as
if he'd just thought of the idea all by himself without any
help from anybody.

"Wait a minute," Cassie said. "I don't want to cause any
more trouble."

"Well, seems to me there's more trouble brewing if you
get an annulment. You're still underage, and when your
cousin finds you, you'll have to go back to Texas." Ash
pondered the situation for a moment or two. "Your marriage might not even be legal if Cecil Gorman is your
guardian, since he didn't exactly give his consent. I'd have
to check the statutes and case law in that area."

Cassie looked frantically at Ted, who was looking stonily
at the pattern of the parquet floor.

"Cassie, I think I can speak for all of us Wellmans when

I say we'd be happy to have you stay with us as long as you need to.'' Ash looked around the room. There were only nods and murmurs of assent.

"Once you're eighteen, Cecil Gorman can't make you go anywhere,'' Ash added. *"Then* you can file for an annulment. You could work for Brock and stay right here—''

"No!'' Cassie interrupted him, but Ash put up his hand to stop her.

"Think about it before you say no, Cassie. It's a pretty good arrangement for the time being. You can stay in Liz's old room, or one of the other bedrooms, for as long as you like. No shortage of bedrooms around this old place.''

"And,'' Maria chimed in, "You can help me with breakfast every morning for your room and board. So it's not as if you'd be accepting charity.'' She had shrewdly guessed one of the things, at least, that was keeping Cassie from accepting their kindness. "The clinic is a nice place to work, and you need a job for six months. You can save some money, and after the annulment you can go anywhere you like.''

"You're a godsend, Cassie, and that's a fact.'' Brock jumped right in to do his part to convince her. "The angels must have heard my prayers last night. Can you start work tomorrow?'' He pulled his wallet from his back pocket and took out two hundred dollars. "Here's an advance on your salary. Ted can drive you into town later today, and you can get some white uniforms.''

"Thank you.'' Cassie swallowed her pride and, all of a sudden, decided to accept. If Ted wasn't going to look at her—well, she didn't have to look at him. She wasn't taking handouts. Here was a job, a family, a home. Even if it was only for six months. Maybe when it was over, she could start college in Texas. Training as a medical secretary had only been the first step to the career in health care she'd planned.

"Let's have some breakfast.'' Alicia's girlish voice and smile were warm. She stood up and walked over to Cassie.

"And then I'll find you a nightie and you can get some rest before you go shopping with Ted. You can have the bedroom next to mine. After riding all the way from Texas in that junky pickup truck, you'll probably sleep the rest of the morning."

"So that's settled. Welcome, Cassie. Now come on and have some breakfast." Bob Wellman's deep voice sounded even warmer than Alicia's. Maria simply beamed.

Bob chuckled as he made his way to the kitchen, his arm around his wife. There hadn't ever been a divorce in the Wellman family. Whether his son was aware of it or not, his fate was sealed. Bob would bet his new silver belt buckle that pretty Cassie was just what Ted need to wake up out of a seven-year sleep, anyway.

Maria smiled up at him. She had won. She had six months to work a little magic. And she intended to make the most of them.

# Chapter Three

"This is my big sister Liz's old room." Alicia opened the door to a bedroom almost the size of the small house Cassie had lived in with her grandmother. "She got married a few years ago, but Momma kept everything pretty much as it was. My room's right across he hall if you ever need anything. Or just want to talk sometime."

"Thank you," Cassie said shyly. She looked around.

The furniture was white wicker, with cushions of white eyelet lace. There were touches of pastel colors everywhere—in the bedspread, the throw pillows, the silk wallpaper, and the drapes covering French doors that led out onto one of the balconies Cassie had seen from the outside.

Even as a little girl, she hadn't believed that real people lived in rooms like this one. Or in houses that looked like pictures in the decorating magazines.

Alicia opened the drapes to a breathtaking view. Dormant trees awaiting the warmth of spring were silhouetted against a wintry blue sky. Cassie shut her eyes and imagined what they would look like when the change of seasons greened the bare branches.

"I've always loved this view. I could have moved over here after Liz married, but it would have taken an army of movers at least a week to get my stuff across the hall," Alicia giggled. "Oh, I nearly forgot. I promised to get you a nightie." She disappeared, leaving the door open behind her.

Cassie touched the silver-handled brush and comb set on the wicker dresser. She was sure if she pinched herself she'd wake up back at Cecil Gorman's ramshackle, run-down farm. All of this would vanish—it had to be only a dream.

Alicia backed into the room, carrying an armload of clothing.

"Here's a nightie, and some underwear. You're about the same size I am so I brought a pair of jeans and a T-shirt. But I think I've got more on top than you so I didn't bring a bra." She piled clothes on the bed and plopped down beside them.

"You didn't have to—" Cassie started to say.

Alicia didn't let her finish. "Hey. I'm going to be your friend. I'm glad to see my brother with some spark again. This family owes you a lot more than a job and a place to stay, Cassie." She smiled again, and Cassie noticed that her smile was exactly like her mother's. And Ted's.

"Okay," Alicia said briskly. "I gotta go. If I don't get a curling iron in this straight hair, I'll look like a mule having a bad hair day." She giggled again. "If you need anything, holler for Momma. We all do. She's too good to us."

She shut the door into the hallway as she left and Cassie opened the door to the bathroom. She turned on the water in the deep, clawfooted, shiny white tub, took a huge, folded pink towel from under the vanity, and set it on the wicker bench at the end of the tub. A big, oval mirror above the vanity reflected a fresh bouquet of daisies and roses. She touched them to see if they were real, then stooped to inhale their scent when she realized that they were.

She dropped her clothes on the floor, and stepped into the most luxurious bath she'd ever had, and thought about the morning. Breakfast had been a big family affair with both brothers and their wives, as well as Ted's parents, and a host of other relatives who'd driven by to meet Cassie and join them at the table.

The lively Wellman clan had gotten right into catching up on the news about Cassie, but Ted had sat at the other end of the table and ignored her completely. Lord, he must be as angry as a wet hen in the middle of a rain storm. He'd thought—and he'd told Cassie while they were driving up—that his Uncle Ash would have papers ready to be signed and he'd be a free man again, just like that. But he was still legally married and it wouldn't be over for six months. She had to admit, if she'd been in his shoes, she would have been standing in the middle of that oak dining table pitching a first-class hissy fit.

Cassie soaked happily for quite a while, until the bath-water turned cold, and the bubbles went flat. She shivered, jumped out of the tub, and wrapped the huge pink towel around her. She remembered Alicia saying that Ted had some spark again, and wondered what she'd meant by that. That sadness Cassie had sensed about him—well, she wondered about that, too. It just might have something to do with why these people were being so nice.

The Wellmans didn't have to do all this for her. No one had ever done so much.

It seemed as if she'd just nestled into the oversized pillow on the bed, and pulled the crisp, white sheets up to her chin and dozed off . . . when the door to the bedroom eased open.

"I hate to wake you," Maria said gently, "but if you're going to buy uniforms for work tomorrow, you'll have to wake up now. Brock keeps the clinic open on New Year's Day." Maria looked at her watch. "It's three-thirty now and the stores are closing early for New Year's Eve," she added.

"Well, hell's bells!" Cassie threw back the covers and hopped out of bed. "Oh, I'm so sorry," she blushed. "Excuse my language, Mrs. Wellman."

Maria laughed, a full, rich laugh that made Cassie smile. "I used to say that when I was a girl in southern Texas, back before I married Bob. My mother used to frown at me and tell me I'd never find a husband if I didn't clean up my language."

"So you grew up in Texas, too?" Cassie pulled Ted's T-shirt over her head and slipped into the jeans Alicia had brought her earlier.

"Yes, I did. But that's a story for another day. For now, you've got to go with your new husband to buy uniforms." Maria straightened the bed as she talked. "I'm glad you decided to stay, Cassie. And please call me Maria. Or Momma, the way Ted does."

"Ye-es," Cassie said slowly. "I appreciate your taking me in—you don't know how much. But I don't plan to impose on your kindness any longer than I have to. Or Ted's. I don't think of him as my husband, you see."

"I do," Maria said simply. She patted the pillows one more time and waved as she left.

"Well, hell's bells," Cassie said again. That sweet lady seemed to *still* like the idea that she and Ted were really married. Was this whole family just plumb crazy?

Ted was waiting for her in the living room. "Ready?" he said flatly.

"I suppose," she answered calmly, not wanting to irk him more than she already had by agreeing to stay. He led the way out the door and to his white pickup, which had a royal blue interior that Cassie hadn't noticed in the half-light of dawn. He didn't talk on the way to town so she didn't either.

He nosed his truck into a parking place in front of a clothing store and turned to look out the side window. The cold was biting, and there wasn't anybody to look at on the streets of Maysville, as far as Cassie could see.

"Are you coming inside with me?" she asked.

"Nope," he answered.

Cassie felt unexpectedly nervous. It had been a long time since she'd been inside a store, other than the pawnshop where she'd hocked her mother's wedding rings. The clerks in this place probably knew Ted well—they probably knew everybody in this small town. She wouldn't mind having him along to introduce her.

"Why not?" she asked tentatively.

"I don't need a uniform. I'm not going to work for Uncle Brock tomorrow morning," he said bluntly. "I'm going to spend a quiet New Year's Eve with my folks tonight and I'm sleeping late tomorrow morning."

Plans that didn't seem to include her, Cassie noted.

"Suit yourself," she retorted, slamming the truck door and storming into the store. So he was mad that she hadn't refused Brock's offer of a job and hitchhiked down the highway. When he'd wanted to play the hero and rescue the fair maiden, he'd been more than kind. But when he was done playacting, he quickly lost interest, Cassie now saw. It was evident he hadn't planned on her staying around to be a thorn in his side for six months until she turned eighteen.

Well, he didn't have any choice in the matter, because she didn't have a choice, when it came right down to it.

"May I help you?" A snooty, over-thirty, overweight, and overly made-up sales clerk approached. The tone of her voice said Cassie was only one step up from being a worm and the sales clerk was only one step away from sprouting wings of gold.

"Yes, ma'am," Cassie said, politely enough. "I need to buy some uniforms. White ones for a doctor's office. Do you stock anything like that?"

"At the back, on the round rack. Dressing room is over

there." The sales clerk pointed with the long, sharp fingernail of her pinkie.

Cassie picked up two pairs of size seven white slacks and tops to match and took them to the dressing room. She took off her clothes and stood in front of the mirror, not believing her reflection. She was so thin the uniforms hung on her frame like a bed sheet on a broomstick. She'd always been petite and slightly built, but she hadn't realized just how lean she'd become over the past six months. The meals she'd missed and the Gormans' regimen of unrelenting work had made her downright skinny.

She pulled her jeans and T-shirt back on, gathered up the uniforms, and padded back to the rack in her socks to find something smaller. The sales clerk and her new customer didn't hear Cassie as she flipped through the rack looking for the same style in a smaller size, but she couldn't help hearing them. The customer's high-pitched, nasal voice was impossible to ignore.

"Well, I heard it at the beauty shop this morning," the customer said breathlessly. "Ted Wellman just up and got married all of a sudden. My cousin Milly said that Doctor Wellman told her that a new person was coming to work at the clinic tomorrow. They're always short on staff on New Year's Day. Everyone's sleeping something off, I guess. Velma, didn't you say his new wife was over there looking at uniforms?"

Cassie stood very still behind the rack, which was just tall enough to hide her.

The witchy sales clerk launched into a meanspirited monologue of her own.

"She ain't much to look at. Kinda plain and skinny as a rail fence," the clerk said haughtily. "She's just Texas white trash, from what I hear. Those Wellman men are supposed to be smart, but I don't think so. Bob, Brock, and Ash ain't got a lick of sense between them. Why should Ted be any different? He's Bob's son, after all."

"Well, I guess you're right. Why did he marry a girl like

that if he didn't have to? Know what I mean?'' The customer cackled unpleasantly.

Cassie was furious. These two biddy hens seemed to have nothing better to do than disparage a family that had shown her every kindness. She hadn't known the Wellmans for very long, but no one—*no one*—was going to say anything bad about them or Ted while Cassie was close enough to hear it.

She took two more pairs of size three pants and two more matching tops from the rack, and didn't take the time to try them on. She marched up to the register and put the garments down on the countertop.

''I also need a pair of white nurse's shoes,'' Cassie said frostily, glaring at the clerk.

''What size?'' the woman snapped.

''Six,'' Cassie snapped back.

The sales clerk went around the end of the counter and picked out a shoe box with the right number on the end. Without another word, she punched the buttons on the cash register. ''That will be one hundred dollars and fifty-nine cents,'' she said prissily, handing the register tape to Cassie as if it were a dead fish. She stuffed Cassie's purchases carelessly into a printed plastic shopping bag.

''Does Ted Wellman have an account in this store?'' Cassie asked.

''Of course he does,'' the clerk said.

''Well, since I'm the skinny girl from Texas he married yesterday, you can go ahead and put all this on his charge account. And don't ask me for I.D. because I know you know who I am. I heard everything you said about me.'' Cassie raised her voice so that the customer who'd been gossiping about her could hear, too. ''And while you're at it, let me give you some advice. If I ever hear you and that other old hen bad-mouth my husband, his relatives or me ever again, I intend to slap you silly!''

Then, with an icy glare that would have frozen off Lucifer's horns on a hot July day in hell, Cassie picked up her bag of clothes, and walked out the front door.

She looked back when she was outside to see the clerk and the customer staring out the front window at her, their eyes round and their mouths hanging open wide enough to catch dragonflies. Cassie hopped into Ted's white pickup truck, slid across the seat, put her arms around Ted's neck, and pulled his mouth down to hers for a kiss that came close to knocking the socks off all four of their collective feet.

That kiss surprised him. Ted had just been considering apologizing for his rudeness that morning—after all, it wasn't her fault that his family had asked her to stay. If he had to guess, he'd say she'd forgiven him in advance for some reason.

Cassie broke off the kiss finally, and reached in her pocket. She set five twenty-dollar bills, one ten, and a single on the console between them. "Next time you go in there, pay your bill, and keep the change," she told him. "I used your charge account. They seemed to know I was the new Mrs. Wellman."

Ted thought about that for a moment.

"Okay. Is that why I got a kiss?" he asked cautiously.

"Oh, I don't know," Cassie said. "Let's just say you're a whole lot nicer than some people around here. And you've got plenty of sense, no matter what some people say. After all, you picked me to be your wife—right?"

"Looks like I did." Suddenly uncomfortable with the curious stares of the store clerk and her customer, Ted detached Cassie's arms from around his neck and slid away from her on the seat. He stared out the window once more, tapping a hand on the steering wheel.

"And it looks like we're going to be together for longer than I thought. Even though we don't know each other at all."

"Well, I can return these right now and you can drive me

to Oklahoma City and never have to see me again—'' Cassie began.

"No. You need a place and my family seems to like you."
He raked a strong hand through his thick hair, making it stand on end. Cassie would've poked fun at him for it if his expression hadn't been so serious.

"Sorry, Cassie. This just isn't how I expected to start the new year."

# *Chapter Four*

Her green eyes were open at five A.M. just like always, and Cassie hopped out of the luxurious bed, ready for her favorite time of the day. She slipped into the faded jeans she'd worn the day she'd escaped Cecil Gorman, pulled on a pair of white socks, and opened the closet to find a T-shirt. There was a wonderful array of clothing. Alicia had brought something almost every day that week, always with a similar explanation: the item was too small or she didn't wear it any more.

Somehow a brand-new, gorgeous green jacket and matching short, straight skirt had showed up in the closet on Saturday. When Cassie had asked Maria about it, she'd said the gypsy fairies must have put in there in the night. Evidently the gypsy fairies had known how good Cassie would look in it when she went to church with the family the next day. Cassie figured gypsy fairies probably had slightly graying dark hair and wonderfully warm brown eyes, but she accepted the suit with good grace.

Cassie straightened her bed and bounded down the stairs in her socks to help Maria fix breakfast. The holidays were over, and a comfortable household routine had been reestablished. She'd lived in the house for a week, and already she felt that her time there would be too short.

The day would come when she would have to sever her relationship with the Wellmans, as well as Ted, and she wasn't looking forward to it.

There would be sweet memories, but the separation was going to be painful. Cassie already cared too deeply for this family to want to leave them, ever. Ted—well, she wasn't so sure about Ted . . .

Maria stood at the counter with her back to Cassie, already preparing breakfast, and Cassie sneaked up and startled her with a quick kiss.

"Oh! Good morning, Cassie." She stirred biscuit dough in a large crockery bowl. "Never seen anyone wake up so full of energy and with such a beautiful smile. You're a ray of sunshine even before the sun comes up," she added.

Maria was as comfortably dressed as Cassie, in loose-fitting jeans, a white cotton shirt, and a white bibbed apron tied around her waist. Her hair was tied back with a bright red ribbon.

"Thank you." Cassie beamed. She took a stack of plates to the table. "How many this morning?"

"Brock's not here. He left about an hour ago to deliver a baby at the hospital. Ash and Maggie will be here soon. Liz and Rich aren't coming out in the cold this morning. So that makes seven of us at the table." Maria dumped the dough onto a floured board, kneaded it a few times, and began pinching off perfectly uniform biscuits. She put them on a baking sheet one by one and slid it into the preheated oven.

Cassie opened the silver flatware chest on top of the sideboard and counted out forks, knives, and spoons. She pulled out a drawer and took out the placemats Maria liked to use for breakfast. The mats were sunshine yellow linen with big appliquéd sunflowers. Maria told her that first day that breakfast was the time to set the mood for the whole day—yellow linen would brighten the table, good food would satisfy the appetite, and loving family would make the heart smile.

"Why do Ash and Maggie drive over here for breakfast?" she asked. "They must have to get up awfully early."

"Maggie can't cook," Maria laughed.

"Really?"

"No." Maria's expression grew serious. "Maggie's a fine cook. It wasn't until the accident that they started to eat with us. It was to help all of us get through the days at first. We needed to be together. The accident happened a long time ago, but we still prefer to eat together as often as we can."

Cassie paused. Something *had* happened to this family —or to Ted—and it must have been something dreadful, judging by the change in Maria's tone of voice.

"What accident? What happened?" Cassie put the knives on the right side of the plates and started distributing spoons to each place setting.

Maria kept working but didn't answer. She had never had to tell the story before, but at least Ted wasn't up yet. No one dared to mention the accident in Ted's presence for fear it would send him over an invisible, frightening line. It had just seemed best never to mention it again. After all, it had been seven years ago . . .

Maria composed herself, trying to think of the best way to answer Cassie's question. This lovely young girl had seen enough trouble in her life—and yet, if she cared for Ted, the accident that had scarred him was something she would have to understand. Maria knew that her son had never talked about it to anyone.

"Ted told me that you once said if you are going to understand today, then you must know yesterday. So I will begin with yesterday," Maria finally said, just when Cassie thought she was going to completely ignore her question.

She watched Maria take the golden-brown biscuits out of the oven and set them aside to cool on top of the stove to keep them warm, and then crack eggs into a cast iron skillet sizzling with melted butter.

The ordinary morning task of preparing breakfast was a comforting ritual that Maria knew would help her get through the extraordinary task of telling Cassie what had happened to Ted—and their family—on that terrible day.

"You know, Cassie, that Liz is my oldest child. Two years after she was born I had the twins. John and Ted," Maria began.

"Ted has a twin brother?" Cassie wasn't sure she'd heard right.

"Yes," Maria answered, then corrected herself. "He had a twin. He and John were so close we often wondered if it took both of them to make one son. They took their first steps on the same day, they said the same first words on the same day. They laughed together, and when one of them got hurt they both cried. When they were older, they worked for their father and saved their money until they could buy shotguns to go deer hunting. They were only fourteen. The night before their first hunt they couldn't even sleep, they were so excited." She paused. "John and Ted got up before daylight and went out to the woods. Cassie, this was seven years ago—" her voice broke, "But to Ted, it is still as if it happened yesterday."

Maria took a deep breath and sat down in a kitchen chair to continue her story.

"John had climbed a tree to look around for deer and Ted had gone a little farther into the woods. Ted heard a shot and went back . . . to find his brother. John's shotgun had fired accidentally when he'd lowered it to the ground and it killed him instantly." She paused, fighting back tears. "Ted carried his body home and went right back out the door. Bob followed him, in shock, but Ted didn't even know his father was there.

"Ted beat those two guns around the tree until they were useless, and then he screamed at the tree until there was no voice left in him. When he came home he didn't say a word and he didn't cry. One half of him was gone forever and only half of Ted lived on."

"Oh, my God . . ." Cassie's voice quivered.

Maria wiped her tears with a corner of her apron. "Cassie, a mother is never prepared to lose a child. We know that we will someday lose our parents and we are able to grieve for them when they are gone. But to lose a child is unnatural, and the grief is unnatural, so it never goes away. But Ted's grief is twice as bad, because his other self—his twin—is not there anymore. It is only since he brought you home that there is some life in him. We are grateful, Cassie," she said quietly. "But we never talk of this around Ted and you must never—" She stopped, as Ted came through the dining room door. Cassie wondered if he had been listening from the other room.

"Where's Uncle Brock?" Ted asked. "He always beats me to the breakfast table."

"Gone to the hospital to deliver a baby," Maria said, in as normal a voice as she could manage. "Go shake Alicia out of bed. I hear Ash and Maggie in the driveway now. And holler at your Poppa. He's probably still reading the paper in our bedroom."

"Okay," Ted said. He poked his head back around the doorjamb to talk to Cassie. "I guess you'll need a ride to Brock's office this morning. I have to go to the lumberyard at eight-thirty. I can take you."

"Sure. Thanks."

Alicia wandered in sleepily ten minutes after everyone else had begun eating. She was a beauty and if she'd been a foot taller she probably could have been a model. But she was just under five feet tall. Long black hair flowed down her back and her eyes were so brown they were almost black. Her skin had a permanent tan and her delicate face had dark eyebrows, long lashes, and a full mouth. In her first year at college, she'd already acquired more suitors than she knew what to do with.

"Mornin'," she mumbled. "Where's Uncle Brock?"

"Out at the cabbage patch finding a baby," Ted said between bites of biscuit.

"Oh, then you need a ride." Alicia nodded toward Cassie and reached for a biscuit herself.

"I'm going to the lumberyard so I'll drive her in," Ted said quickly, and Alicia winked at Cassie.

Ted wolfed his food, trying not to look at his—wife. He was sort of getting a little more used to that idea. Cassie looked incredibly pretty today. Was it his imagination, or had she already filled out some? Momma's home cooking could put curves on any girl.

At eight-fifteen he called up the stairs to tell her he was ready when she was. Cassie quickly ran a comb through her curls and clamped a big white barrette at the nape of her neck. Butterflies the size of buzzards were having a party in her stomach. Both Alicia and Maria had hinted that Ted had changed since she'd been around.

But why?

Cassie's arrival had been a complication he'd never anticipated. But then he could've dropped her off in Oklahoma City and not ever brought her home, if he truly hadn't wanted to be involved with her. Ash could've arranged the annulment even if she hadn't stayed with them. But the more Cassie thought about what had happened, the more she realized that Ted's affectionate family had drawn Cassie into their affectionate circle before she'd had a chance to think.

It was clear enough from what his mother had told her that the Wellmans were close—and they had drawn even closer together to help Ted and each other through the trauma of John's accidental death. They were just warmhearted folks who naturally looked out for each other—and for other people, too. Cassie would bet anything that when she'd told Ted she wasn't just a stray puppy he could

bring home, she had hit on a hidden tenderness that he
had vowed never to feel again.

Cassie had a hunch that this closeknit clan might even
have protected him too much. Unable to express his grief,
unable even to talk about it, Ted seemed to have shut
down all his feelings.

Losing the person who was closest to him—his twin
brother—*had* made him seem only half alive, as his
mother had said.

Out of kindness and love, his family had respected his
feelings and left him alone, locked in his grief. But life
went on. It had to. Accepting its challenges and hurts
wasn't easy, as Cassie knew all too well.

How or why Ted had ever decided to take a chance on
*her* and say anything as risky as the simple words, "I do,"
was utterly beyond her comprehension.

Cassie supposed Ted wouldn't pull a stunt like that for
just anybody. But why her? She'd have to figure that out
for herself. She sighed. Ted didn't seem inclined to talk
about it. Or anything else . . .

He called up the stairs again, somewhat testily, to ask if
she was ready yet, and Cassie finished fussing with her hair.
He certainly was every bit as impatient as a real husband,
she thought, amused.

"Coming!" she called back and left the room.

When she descended the staircase, he was waiting for
her, with a big smile on his face for some reason. Which
was a beginning. No telling where they might end up.

Cassie had no idea of how good she looked to him,
and how much her presence in the house brightened his
mornings. But Ted knew. Even if he didn't always want to
show it.

# Chapter Five

Ted heard the clock chime once. Then, an hour later, he heard it chime again. He was no closer to coming to grips with his feelings than he had been four hours earlier when he'd first laced his hands behind his head on the pillow and began thinking. The ceiling had become a big screen television set for his imagination.

There was Cassie in those faded jeans and white socks, carrying a big platter of ham and biscuits to the breakfast table. There she was when he took her to Brock's office, in her white uniform with her curls neatly pulled back in a barrette, but one red curl was always struggling to escape. And there she was in that green suit that showed off her beautiful legs.

Cassie fit into his family as if she'd been specially groomed for the part, and she was starting to fit into his heart more than he wanted anyone to fit there ever again.

He mentally changed stations on his imaginary television set, and suddenly there was his twin John, laughing at him for losing the race when they got off the school bus. Then the two of them had chicken pox and were miserable . . .

and then there was John, lifeless, under the tree where Ted had found him. Ted wept as he remembered the day of his brother's death, and the hurt deep in his heart tightened its cold grip.

No, he'd been right when he'd decided not to love anyone, not even his family, ever again . . .

The image of Cassie came back to him, as she'd looked when she'd come flying out of the clothing store and slid across the front seat of his truck to kiss him. Damn that sassy little Texas spitfire for making him yell, making him smile, and for making him think about things like love again.

Not that she really treated him differently from the other members of the family, maybe not even as warmly.

He supposed he deserved as much. He'd been careful not to give her any special treatment. Not after the way she'd set him up, and then gotten his family all involved. Whose side were they on, anyway? Not his, Ted was positive about that.

He'd have to look out for himself and keep his distance if he wanted to keep his sanity. Other than that one kiss she'd planted on him outside the clothing store, they hadn't touched each other, and Ted intended to keep it that way.

Ted reached over and picked up a quarter, a dime, a nickel, and a penny from the nightstand beside his bed. He smiled in the darkness and held the cool change next to his cheek. "Pay your bill and keep the change," she'd said. Well, forty-one cents was the change.

It occurred to him belatedly that Cassie had bought enough in the way of uniforms to let him know she planned on working for his Uncle Brock for a while.

Which promised to make life interesting—if not peaceful. Ted remembered the electricity between them when he'd kissed her on their wedding day and the jolt he'd felt when she'd kissed him in front of the store. Ted wondered . . . had she felt the same way?

He should get out more, he thought. Date somebody else, he told himself without thinking. Ted smiled ironically. He couldn't date. He was a married man, and the whole town knew it.

Ted considered the possibility that, deep down inside, he had actually wanted to marry Cassie. There was such a thing as love at first sight, he thought. Maybe sometimes the people who fell in love that way didn't even know it.

The clock chimed again, three times. His late granddaddy had told him once that everyone should just slow down, take life easy, and quit running in circles. Well, the first two recommendations weren't too difficult to follow . . . but controlling his mind to keep it from running in circles and coming back to Cassie all the time . . . now, that might be next to impossible to accomplish.

Ted reconsidered her kisses. He had kissed more than his share of girls, but until Cassie had blazed into his life, he'd felt as if he was simply doing what was expected of him. *She* made him feel almost—hungry for more.

His stomach rumbled, reminding him that it had been an eternity since supper. At least that was one hunger he could satisfy now. He remembered seeing a double-layer chocolate cake in the kitchen, and his mouth began watering with thoughts of cake and a tall glass of icy cold milk. Eating was as good a way as any not to think about her.

Ted flipped on a light and scrounged around in a drawer for some sweatpants. He went noiselessly downstairs, in socks and sweats, but barechested.


Cassie tossed and turned in her sleep, dreaming that she was running, running, and going nowhere. Her feet were like lead and adrenaline was racing through her veins. That awful sheriff was chasing her, gaining ground, and she kept running in slow motion. If he caught her, he would take her back to Cecil and she knew she could never get away.

Returning from the kitchen, Ted heard a soft moan when he started past her bedroom door. Before he took another step, she cried out in her sleep, begging and sobbing.

"Help me . . . please . . ."

He pushed the door open quickly, half-expecting to find an intruder in the room. She was fighting the covers and seemed to be trying to run, even though she was flat on her back. Her face glistened with tears and her hair was limp with sweat. She had to be having one hell of a nightmare.

"Cassie?" he whispered. He sat down on the edge of the bed and shook her gently.

"Don't hurt me," she whimpered, trying to pull the covers over her head.

"Cassie, wake up."

"Help me . . ." she sobbed.

He gathered her in his arms and sat on the edge of the bed while he rocked her back and forth as if she were a tiny baby. "Wake up, Cassie. Honey, it's only a dream . . ." He rubbed her back and whispered into her hair.

"Ted?" She woke up a little, wondering just what he was doing in her room. Her nightmare was still vivid enough for her to instinctively turn to his comforting warmth. She snuggled down into the dark, soft hair on his chest, without it seeming wrong at all.

"You had a bad dream . . . you cried out," he explained in a whisper, hoping she wouldn't hear the double-time his heart was doing. Holding her so close felt incredibly good . . . like nothing he had ever felt before. She warmed his body—and his lonely soul.

"It was horrible," she sobbed again. "I was running and running and I couldn't get anywhere. Couldn't move . . ."

"Just a bad dream," Ted murmured and pushed her damp hair back from her forehead. He didn't mean to kiss her, but one second he was looking at her tear-streaked face and the next he was tasting the salt on her lips.

She responded eagerly, with a drowsy hunger of her own. The shelter of his strong arms relaxed her, and his gentle kiss seemed to banish her frightening dream of pursuit and capture.

Cassie opened her eyes, and woke up all the way, looking at him with wide eyes. The intimacy of their embrace, his semi-naked state, and her ardent response, must be giving him the wrong idea entirely.

But why did it feel so right?

Cassie had been kissed before, by the only boy brave enough to try it behind Cecil's back, but it hadn't felt like this. Warm, trusting, loving, sensual . . . Oh, Lord. This was farther than she wanted to go right now. Cassie sat up and wriggled out of his arms. Ted looked disappointed and relieved all at the same time.

And maybe just a little bit confused. She couldn't blame him. Cassie reached out and patted his cheek tenderly, and they sat there, awkwardly silent for a moment or two.

"Um—" Cassie said.

"I didn't mean—" Ted said quickly. "I didn't mean to interrupt you. What were you going to say?"

"Nothing."

"I guess I shouldn't have come in."

"That's all right. You—we—didn't do anything wrong."

"I was on my way to the kitchen," he said, which was true enough. "I was—hungry. There's still cake and milk." He stumbled over his explanation, feeling like a fool. "Want to go downstairs with me and have some?"

She nodded. "Maybe I'll have some coffee instead." Feeling still half-asleep, she didn't quite trust herself to be alone with him. Cuddling up had felt like heaven—the kind of heaven she'd never imagined she'd find. Cassie had concentrated on working hard for most her young life, and romance hadn't been part of her game plan. When he wasn't around, she didn't think about Ted too much. Well, not all day, anyway.

But when he was close to her, as he was now, the romantic

notions she was able to dismiss in broad daylight seemed dangerously real. And almost intoxicating.

A cup of good strong coffee would definitely do her good.

Ted tried not to look her up and down. The situation they'd found themselves in seemed definitely compromising, and her sleepwear was doing wonders for his sex drive, even though it didn't show all that much of her.

But she looked adorable. Cassie had on pink flannel pajamas that were at least three sizes too big for her. The sleeves and pants legs were rolled up, and the top fell practically to her knees. Ted thought she looked a little less scared, especially once he got her into the kitchen's enveloping warmth, and he was secretly pleased that he'd been able to reassure her.

Ted helped himself to another slab of chocolate cake and poured a glass of milk while she microwaved a cup of water for instant coffee. "Have bad dreams often?" he asked. He perched on a stool beside the bar dividing the dining room and the kitchen. He'd been careful not to touch her or brush against her as they'd moved about preparing their snacks, but it hadn't cooled him off a whole hell of a lot.

Making small talk wasn't going to be easy.

Cassie didn't seem to notice his discomfort, fortunately. She thought for a moment before answering his question.

"Oh—I've had them since I had to go live with Cecil. And after I ran away. They seem silly when I wake up, but they're awfully scary when I'm asleep. Do your dreams ever bother you?"

The kind of dreams he'd been having about Cassie most definitely did bother him. But he knew her just well enough to keep his mouth shut about them.

"Oh, sometimes," he said casually. "But not tonight. I was just hungry, that's all."

"Do you get hungry in the middle of the night very

often?'' She stirred her coffee to cool it, and looked at him, wide-eyed.

Ted couldn't stand it. He knew she was just trying to make small talk, just like him, but if she asked him one more leading question, he was going to . . . do nothing. There was nothing he could do.

"Yeah," he said finally, roughing up his hair as if to get rid of the wayward thoughts that wouldn't stop coming. "I get hungry." He poked at his cake with a fork. She looked so sexy he had almost lost his appetite. They had to get onto safer ground. There had to be topics of conversation that didn't sound so suggestive . . . especially when she talked to him in that sleepy-sweet voice. It was a voice that was meant to be heard from one pillow away, and he couldn't take it another second.

"Let's talk about something else," he said briskly.

She raised a quizzical eyebrow. "Okay. Pick a topic."

He talked to her about his brief stint at the agricultural college and his return to his father's business, and the ins and outs of oil well machinery, until her eyes began to glaze over with boredom.

Cassie took the conversational lead then, steering him towards livelier subjects until two hours had passed and they seemed to have talked about everything under the sun. One subject led naturally to another and yet another, until it began to look as if a friendship—and a budding romance—might be born out of a nightmare and a hungry stomach.

There, in the big old farmhouse kitchen, Ted finally confided a lifelong dream of his to Cassie . . . to build his own house someday, on the adjoining land that his father had given him.

A two-storey log cabin, no less.

Cassie smiled. It seemed more like a little boy's odd notion than anything else. She'd never heard of a log cabin that had more than one room, or more than one storey, for that matter. She couldn't resist the temptation to tease him a little.

"A two-storey log cabin? What for? You don't need a house of your own. You'd probably come here to eat anyway." Her eyes were bright with laughter, and Ted felt a little annoyed.

"Oh, I can cook if I have to. It's not all that hard. After all, you and my mother do it every day. How difficult can it be?"

"That's exactly my point. You've never done it for yourself." Cassie's cheeks pinked up. She could feel an argument coming on, and she felt practically powerless to stop it.

"Hey, if nothing else, I can always open up a can of beans."

"Sounds wonderful. Eating beans in your great, big log cabin, all by yourself. How are you ever going to find a woman who'll like living that way?"

"I can manage on my own, thanks."

Cassie couldn't resist another dig.

"Planning to be a hermit, huh?"

"Probably, until I'm about thirty-five."

She studied him for a moment, with her chin propped in her hands and her coffee cup forgotten in front of her.

"What happens when you're thirty-five?"

"I don't know. Just sounds more grown-up than twenty-one, that's all. I figure when I'm thirty-five, I'll know what I want to do, and who I want to really marry, and stuff like that," he finished lamely.

"Ah. A real marriage. To a real wife, right?" Cassie said wryly.

"Yeah. A real wife. What's wrong with that?"

Cassie slid off her stool, and sauntered around the kitchen. Ted couldn't fathom how she could be so annoying and so attractive at the same time—and do it in pajamas that were baggy enough for the center ring.

No question. This girl got to him like nobody ever had.

But he didn't like the way she seemed to be making fun of his dreams for a house, and a life, and a real wife . . . maybe because those dreams had begun to include her.

"What exactly is a 'real' wife, anyway?" Cassie asked pertly. His vision of domestic bliss seemed pretty old-fashioned, if he wanted her opinion. Which she very much doubted he did.

"A real wife would want lots of kids, and she'll love them and she'll love me. And she'll stand on the front porch every day to wave goodbye when I go to work." Ted stubbornly defended his idea of what marriage should be, even though it sounded half-baked, even to him.

"Wait a minute." Cassie held up a palm toward him. "First of all, why does she have to stand on the porch like a puppet and wave to you? She's going to have a hard time doing that with a baby on each hip, and another on the way. What if she wants a career—and children, too? Would you help?"

"I guess so," Ted said cautiously. "As much as I could. But I don't want a woman who thinks more of her damned job than me and the children."

"That won't necessarily be true," Cassie argued. "It's possible for a woman to love her husband and her children, and still hold down a job. There's daycare. Your mother would love to help raise a grandchild."

"I won't have my children in daycare and my mother has raised her kids and she did the best job ever, but she isn't going to raise mine, too."

His voice had risen to just below a yell.

Cassie was well aware that this argument was entirely theoretical—even ridiculous—but she stuck to her guns.

"Don't you yell at me!" she yelled.

"Don't you tell me how to raise my kids!" he yelled even louder.

They were nose to nose, milk and cake and coffee forgotten in the heat of the silly argument.

"Ted Wellman, you don't even have any kids. You aren't

mature enough to be a real father. Or even a real husband.''

''Hush! You're going to wake up the whole damn house!''

Cassie folded her arms across her chest and dropped her voice to no more than a belligerent whisper. ''So?''

He sucked in a deep breath, and tried to stare her down. Lord, but her green eyes were even more gorgeous when she got really mad.

She turned away and wouldn't even look at him. His powerful arms were folded across his chest, and his natural musculature, developed to perfection by hard work in the fields, was unnerving to see. How could a man who had cradled her so tenderly against that very same chest, held her in those arms, yell at her like this?

If either of them had any sense, they would knock off this silly quarrel and just go upstairs and do what came naturally. The sexual tension between them was making them act plumb crazy, and Cassie knew it, young as she was.

She sighed.

Was it worth her while to make him listen to reason? They seemed to have gone well beyond reason, she thought, as she finally met his gaze.

He almost gave in. But some devil in him made him have to have the last word.

''You know something, Cassie? You're too inexperienced to understand anything about love and marriage.''

''I know what I feel,'' she said stubbornly. ''Which is more than you can say.''

She regretted the words the minute they were out of her mouth, but there was no taking them back.

''Don't be so sure of that, Cassie.'' Ted's voice was dangerously, sexily low. ''I know what I feel about you.''

She walked over to him and stood less than an inch away from his half-naked body as if daring him to touch her.

He didn't.

He wouldn't give her that satisfaction. Or the satisfaction of winning this argument.

"It's your bedtime, little girl. Just remember something. You're much too young to be anybody's real wife."

Cassie saw red, and she had the sudden urge to knock him off his feet and into the middle of next week. But she controlled herself somehow, if only for the sake of the rest of the family, who didn't need to hear any of this.

She took a deep breath.

"I may be younger than you, Ted Wellman, but not by much. And I've seen more of life than you will ever see. You don't know everything there is to know, no matter how loudly you yell."

He looked at her without replying. Cassie continued.

"By the way, don't tell me who I am and what I should be. You're not in charge of me, or my life—any more than that tyrant Cecil is."

That stung.

Was she actually comparing him to that nasty man she was afraid of—the one who'd treated her like a slave? Ted *had* been kind, he knew that much. Hadn't he gotten her out of trouble with the law? He'd married her, hadn't he, and wasn't he putting up with a lot of hateful sass right now?

"Oh, quiet down." He was nose to nose with her once more, but she had to stand on her tiptoes to face him down, so Ted figured that gave him a slight advantage. "Don't you compare me to that Cecil. I mean it, Cassie. Damn it all to hell, I've done a lot for you. I don't care how mad you are, don't you dare say I'm like him. Or else."

"Or else what?" she taunted him. "Hellfire, I'll talk as loud as I want!" Her concern for the family was momentarily forgotten. "Ted, you couldn't see my point if you wanted to because whatever I say goes in one ear and out the other. There isn't anything in your hollow head to slow it down. I'm going back to bed. I wouldn't ever be your wife on anything but paper. And I wouldn't wish that awful fate on my worst enemy, either, and that's a fact!''

She stormed out of the kitchen just as the clock chimed five times.

# *Chapter Six*

"Maria, do we have to use the yellow placemats today? I don't feel so cheerful," Cassie said when she set the table for breakfast a couple of days later.

"What has Ted done to make you angry?" Maria asked bluntly.

"How did you know?" Cassie was amazed.

"Because mothers know," Maria said calmly. She didn't add that only a person you care about—or even love—can take the sunshine from your heart. Or that for the past two days Cassie had been as friendly as ever with everyone in the family—but when Ted was there the sparks flew until they were almost visible.

"Your son is a—" Cassie stopped herself. She couldn't bear to tell this wonderful woman just how immature Ted could be, or how protecting him from his feelings for so many years had kept him from growing up.

"My son is a wonderful, caring man who is just learning to love again." Maria finished Cassie's sentence for her to save her new daughter-in-law the trouble of eating a lot of unkind words later.

"Well, it's plain enough that he doesn't love me." As soon as she'd spoken, Cassie wished she could take the words back and choke on them. All the Wellmans knew that Ted thought she was too young to be a "real wife" by now. What did she care whether he loved her or not?

Maria bit the inside of her lower lip to keep from laughing. So it had been a lover's quarrel after all. She and Maggie had both figured it had to be, but they weren't exactly certain when it happened. How absolutely wonderful!

"Good mornin', Momma." Ted sat down at the table. "Where's Uncle Brock?"

"In the living room with your Poppa, reading the paper. You just walked through there. Didn't you notice them?" Maria loved it.

"Guess I haven't been sleeping so well," he mumbled, rubbing his eyes. "Red placemats? Momma, you know I hate red," Ted grumbled.

"I told Cassie to put red on the table this morning," his mother replied. "Stop complaining. You sound like a little boy," she added, chiding him in a gentle voice. "Run and get Alicia out of bed and tell your dad and Brock that breakfast is ready. I think I just heard Ash and Maggie open the front door."

All three of the Wellman brothers—Bob, Brock, and Ash—came to the table together. Cassie sat across from them, smiling politely while she made small talk and tried desperately to ignore Ted, who sat right beside her this morning.

The telephone rang, providing a merciful interruption in the somewhat strained atmosphere.

Bob grabbed for the extension on the bar, said "Hello," and handed the receiver to Brock. "For you," he said tersely. "So do you think this oil well commission is going to work with us this time?" He continued his business conversation with Ash.

"Hope so."

"Gotta run." Brock dabbed his mouth with a red napkin and left half his breakfast on his plate. "Dorena Jackson is ready to deliver." He dashed out before Cassie could ask him for a ride.

"Where's Alicia?" Maria inquired.

"Note on her door said there were teacher's conferences today and there's no school. She's sleeping 'til noon. Do not disturb," Ted said in a flat voice.

"Excuse me." Cassie laid her napkin beside her plate. Brock had left and Alicia wasn't going to school It would take her at least forty-five minutes to get ready and walk to the clinic, and she would sit on a barbed wire fence before she'd ask Ted to take her to work. She went up the stairs two at a time.

Everyone at the table was quiet until they heard her shut her bedroom door upstairs. Maria looked at Ted. What had he said to hurt Cassie's feelings so? The girl hadn't eaten more than two bites of breakfast in a couple of days now—just when she was beginning to fill out a bit, too.

Ash looked at Ted. Lord, he'd worried about that boy ever since the day they'd called him and said John was dead. Ted had just shut down from that day on. Oh, he'd gotten dutifully through his responsibilities around the farm, and pitched in the family oil business, but his nephew had scarcely shown a flicker of emotion since.

Until the night he'd called Ash from Texas to say he was married all of a sudden, and Ash had heard the excitement in his voice . . . hell, Ash had figured Ted would turn into a cantankerous recluse who would never really trust or love another soul. But Cassie had changed that.

Bob looked at Ted. His only living son was as smart as a bullwhip. He'd taken over the business management of the farm and everything was kept in perfect order. He owned his own equipment, plowed his own land, brought forth bountiful crops . . . but if the boy was so damned smart, why was he cutting off his nose to spite his face? This little redheaded gal his son had rescued had sorta rescued *him*, the way Bob saw it. So he and Cassie had had a little spat. Didn't Ted know how to apologize?

Ted looked up from his plate. "Hey, what'd I do?" he mumbled. "Why is everyone looking at me like that?"

"What did you do to Cassie?" his father asked.

"Huh? Dad, why don't you ask what she did to me?" Ted was upset, and his voice betrayed his feelings.

Maria wanted to cry for joy. Her son, who hadn't raised his voice in years, was actually showing emotion. Even if it was anger, it was still emotion, and it might start the healing process he needed so badly.

"Well, you obviously hurt her feelings," his father pointed out. "What did you two fight about, anyway?"

"We didn't fight." Ted pushed his chair back so fast his napkin fell on the floor and he knocked his juice over. Cassie is as stubborn as a mule—and she's childish. She has to have her way about everything!" He got up and faced his family with an unmistakably mulish expression of his own.

"You're not all that grown-up yourself, you know," his Uncle Ash said. "It's not fair of you to judge her so harshly. You're both kids, really."

Ted glared at him, and the others.

"Thank you everybody, for your unanimous vote of confidence. Just tell me one thing. Why are all of you on *her* side? I'll be damned glad when this six months is over and she gets out of my life."

Ted whacked the back of his chair with enough force to make his hand sting.

"Until then, son, she *is* your wife." Bob suppressed a chuckle. "And she needs a ride to work and she isn't going to beg you. I suppose I could offer her a ride. Or your mother could drive her. At least everyone in Maysville won't see your wife walking to work while you sit here with a brand-new truck, sulking to beat the band."

"Oh, hell." Ted stormed out of the dining room and up the stairs to do his duty . . . and get his family off his back. He rued the day he'd decided to get that snot-nosed redhead out of trouble. Now his whole family was taking her side over his. Ted had been almost ready to admit that he liked having her around—until that fight. She'd taken pains to let him know she wasn't interested in any dream of his. He'd be a gentleman and take the brat to work, though, even if she didn't deserve it. But he damn sure didn't have to enjoy it.

Ted knocked on the door.

No answer.

He knocked again, louder.

There was still no answer.

He slung it open forcefully.

Cassie was standing in front of the balcony doors, with her back to him. She was neatly dressed for work in her all-white uniform, down to the white barrette. But one curl had already escaped and was sneaking around her ear.

"Cassie?" His voice as cold as steel in a January snowstorm.

"What?" She didn't turn around and her voice was even colder than his.

"I've got to go to the lumberyard. I'll give you a ride into work," he stated firmly then started to shut the door.

"You don't have to go to the lumberyard. I'd rather walk anyway."

"You're not going to walk. And that's that."

"Stop, it, Ted." Cassie turned around. Her eyes were red and her mascara ran down her cheeks in dark brown streaks. "Maria probably made you come up here and say you'd take me to work. I know you don't want to drive me. I'll walk every step of the way and you can just go to hell. Or else go wherever it is all you big, mature men go when us children go to work every day."

"Don't be stupid," he snapped.

"I'm not," Cassie's eyes flashed. "You're the stupid one. You wouldn't see the light if the sun dropped out of the sky and landed in your lap."

"I'm not going to fight with you, Cassie. Just be down-stairs and ready on time because I'm takin' you to work whether you like it or not." He shook his finger at her. "And by the way, Momma did not tell me to come up here and say I'd take you to work."

"I don't believe you. You're only polite to me because you're afraid of what your family might say," she snapped. "You don't care about me. You don't care about anyone but yourself."

"Right. You just better be ready by eight-fifteen." Ted slammed the bedroom door with enough force to rattle the windows.

"When pigs fly!" she yelled through the door.

At exactly quarter past eight, Ted left the family office located above the three-car garage and went down the stairs to the living room. Not that he'd done any work in the past hour. He'd propped his feet on the desk and let a glorious feeling of anger take over his entire body and soul.

He didn't even know how good it felt to feel bad until he started analyzing why he wanted to tear something to shreds, why he wanted to throw the glass paperweight at the wall and why he wanted to spank that redhaired peck of trouble he'd brought home.

He was almost as angry as he was the day that damned gun killed his brother. He thought about John and the good times they'd shared, the hurts, the laughter and oddly enough, instead of anger, a feeling of peace enveloped him like a warm blanket. Then Cassie invaded his thoughts and he was angry again. How could a man feel such peace one minute and anger the next? It had been too long since he'd felt anything at all for him to figure it out.

Cassie wasn't waiting in the living room for him.

"Where is she?" he asked his father, who was pretending to read the paper he'd just hidden himself behind. Ted noticed it was upside down.

"Who?" Bob asked innocently.

"Where is Cassie? I told her I would drive her to work," Ted said doggedly.

"She must not have heard you. But everyone at the breakfast table heard you slamming doors and screaming something about her not being stupid. Was that what you said? I couldn't quite hear." Bob coughed to keep the chuckle out of his voice.

"Yeah, that's what I said. Not that I think she's stupid. But she *is* the most exasperating woman I've ever met," Ted said furiously. "I guess she's still pouting up in her room and I'll have to go up there and get her."

Maggie followed Maria out of the kitchen, as both of them wiped their hands on their aprons. "You looking for your wife?" his aunt asked. "You'll probably find her about half a mile from town. She left right after you practically broke the windows in your Momma's house slamming that door so hard."

"Damn it!" Ted growled—but his mother knew he wasn't really talking to her or his aunt. He tore out the front door, jumped into his truck, and slung gravel all over the driveway when he peeled out. He pushed the gas pedal to the floor, let up on it, stomped the clutch and shifted into the next gear, then repeated the procedure until he was racing down the dirt road toward Maysville.

Ted spotted Cassie about a half mile from the clinic, just on the outskirts of town. He left thirty feet of tire marks in the gravel before he came to a screeching halt behind her. Before she could turn around he was out of the truck and standing in front of her.

"I told you I'd take you to work," he yelled.

"And I told you not to bother," she yelled right back. "Now hop right back in your shiny new truck and go back to the office your daddy set up to keep you busy, and do whatever rich little boys do. I've got a real job to get to."

Ted opened the door to his truck, picked up a length of rope from behind the seat and started toward her. Cassie saw what he was holding and took off in a dead run. She was little but she was a country girl and she could outrun this big ox any day of the week. She might look like the wrath of God had descended upon her when she made it to the clinic, but she'd have a high color in her cheeks, that was for sure.

Ted's rope floated out of the air like a halo and lassoed her, pinning her arms to her sides. Before she could take another step, think another thought, or even say a cuss word, he had it looped around her three times and tied it in a knot. He threw her over his shoulder, even though she was kicking him hard enough to cause bruises. Ted simply didn't seem to care. He opened the passenger side of the truck and plopped Cassie down on the front seat so hard she had trouble catching her next breath.

"You . . . you . . ." she panted. It was impossible to find a word mean enough to throw at him.

"I told you I was going to drive you," he said quietly. "Still want to argue about it?"

She decided not to give him the further satisfaction of an argument, and silently cursed the day she'd laid eyes on him in the bus station diner.

A few minutes later he parked the pickup in front of the clinic, took his time walking around the truck, opened the passenger door slowly and picked Cassie up as carelessly as if she'd been a bag of seed potatoes instead of a woman.

"You put me down right now and untie me," she warned him.

"I'll put you down inside the clinic, just like I said I'd do," Ted retorted.

And that's what he did. In front of the nurse, whose eyes were the size of saucers. In front of Dr. Brock Wellman, who could not keep the grin off his face. In front of the nasty customer who'd gossiped about her in the clothing store back when and who couldn't believe her good luck at seeing Cassie again—in a highly embarrassing situation.

Ted untied her, held her arms down to her sides so she

couldn't slap him, and gave her a kiss that rocked her heart, her mind, and her body.

"Have a good day, Cassie," he said casually, as if he had done nothing out of the ordinary at all.

Ted whistled as he walked out of the clinic with the rope draped over his shoulder, and Cassie stared after him, speechless with indignation.

# *Chapter Seven*

Before Ted came in from the fields, Cassie finished helping Maria with supper and escaped to her bedroom with a thick romance novel. She knew when he arrived because she could hear the deep tone of his voice floating up the stairs and through her bedroom door. Maria told him to put his supper in the microwave to warm it up, and Cassie irrationally hoped that his chicken-fried stead would be tough, his gravy would have lumps in it big enough to gag him, and that Maria served it all to him on a red placemat.

The nurse at the clinic had giggled all day about the way that idiot had tied her up and delivered her to work. The mere memory of it was almost as mortifying as the actual experience had been.

Now it was all over Maysville that they had had a typical newlywed fight and Ted had won.

That was the part she hated most . . . he had *won*. And that he had kissed her as if it would make everything just wonderful and left whistling. Well, it damned sure wasn't wonderful and even if he sent a choir of angels to sing his apologies, she would never, ever forgive him for this humiliation. She'd be thrilled when the next five months were over and she could go back to—it suddenly hit her that she had nowhere to go back to.

Ted sat down to a warmed-over meal served up on a red placemat with a red napkin under his silverware. His mother knew he hated that color, he thought irritably. She'd set his plate that way to let him know she wasn't pleased with him. Ted knew very well why, but he wasn't about to traipse up those damn stairs and apologize to Cassie just so he wouldn't have to eat on red placemats.

For the next two weeks, Ted deliberately worked in the office or on his land until after dark and after supper, and made do with microwaved leftovers. Cassie helped Maria, worked at the clinic, and read romance novels in her room. By the time she finished seven of them, she was so tired of happy-ever-after that she thought she would throw up if she read the first page of another one. She missed watching television in the living room. She missed helping Alicia memorize her Latin declensions. She missed sneaking peeks at Ted.

But wild horses couldn't have dragged her down the stairs to rejoin the family, because she hadn't done one thing wrong. Ted had to come to her and say he was sorry for humiliating her, or she'd stay in this room until spring came, and she could sign the divorce papers that would set her free. Maybe she would file for an annulment *and* a divorce, just to be sure she was rid of him.

Cassie reminded herself that spring was just around the corner.

# *Chapter Eight*

It was a glorious Sunday in February, not too hot, not too cold, but one of those just-right days which incubated an ailment called spring fever. Ted knew for a fact that he was suffering from it. His late granddaddy had always told him that spring fever made old men think of seed potatoes and onion plants, and young men dream of love. He'd added that there was no known cure. Well, if that was all that was the matter with him today, Ted thought glumly . . . he'd get over it.

After church that morning, Ted and Cassie were separated by family members who acted like they hadn't seen them in months. Ash suddenly needed to talk about a strange noise in his truck, and Ash's wife took Cassie aside to compliment her on her chic green suit, and ask in guarded whispers if she and Ted had patched up their quarrel. Ted heard the question his aunt whispered—the woman could whisper louder than anybody—but not Cassie's reply. He turned to his uncle, and scowled.

"So have you and Cassie kissed and made up?" Ash leaned against the gleaming front grille of his black truck, and surveyed the people chatting in groups on the lawn in front of the church.

Ted ignored the question.

"What's the matter with your truck, Ash?"

"Nothing." Ash grinned. "I just wanted to talk to you away from the womenfolks. But it's no use. You're hellbent on ignoring me—and her. Too bad, Ted. If you don't want that pretty little woman, someone else is going to snap her up."

"They're welcome to her. I don't want her. I don't even *like* her most of the time, Ash."

His uncle looked at him shrewdly. "Something tells me you're in love with her, Ted," he said finally. "Are you?"

"Love that redheaded hellcat?" Ted laughed. "Falling in love with a five foot rattlesnake would be a lot safer."

Ash sighed. "She sure does have spirit. That's why we all like her so much. Well, see you later. Maggie's cooked up a ham the size of this truck and enough sweet potatoes to feed an army. You'd think the whole town was coming to Sunday dinner, instead of just us Wellmans."

"Last time I counted us Wellmans, I lost count," Ted said crossly. "There's too many, and none of them are on my side. I'm thinking of seceding and starting my own branch of the family."

"Really?"

Ash would've liked to ask a question or two on that subject, but his nephew was already headed for the parking lot.


Ted considered his uncle's words very carefully on the drive home and dismissed the idea that he could ever fall in love with that Cassie O'Malley. It wasn't possible. Or even practical. Even if he was already married to her. He turned on the radio to his favorite country music station, and listened to a recent hit by a singer who had to have been married to a little hellcat just like her.

The woman in the song had thrown most everything the singer had owned on the back forty and given the rest to charity. Life with Cassie might be a lot like that, Ted mused. One thing for sure—it would never be dull. He wouldn't ever have time to sit and grow scar tissue over his heart the way he'd done for the past seven years. She'd keep him on his toes for the rest of his days if they stayed married—and then she'd probably follow him right into eternity and tell St. Peter how to run heaven.

One minute Ted was listening to the song and the next, a car was coming straight at him, driving in the wrong lane. He could see the woman at the wheel frantically trying to get control of it, and the children crowded into the back seat. Then he saw pieces of rubber flying, and he realized her tire had blown. The disabled car got closer and closer and he had to jerk his wheel hard to the left to get in the other lane and give the woman room to pass him. Just as he got his truck straightened out, his left front wheel ran off a low shoulder and he lost control.

The scene played before his eyes in slow motion. He whipped the wheel around, and then the woman passed him, narrowly missing hitting his fender. Then the truck went out of control. Ted slammed into a telephone pole and his head hit the dashboard and bounced back to strike the rear window. Something was hurting his leg and his arm felt cold and wet and it hurt like blazes. And then there was darkness . . .

Maggie hummed softly, pleased with how well everything had turned out. She'd had the table set before she'd left for church that morning. The ham was cooked to perfection with a brown sugar and mustard glaze studded with pineapple chunks, and all the side dishes were ready. Everyone was there except Ted—she figured he had stopped at home. Getting him to wear a suit to church was as far as that boy would ever go . . . he must have decided to change into jeans before Sunday dinner. Unless he hadn't remembered dinner was at her house this Sunday . . .

The phone rang and Alicia picked it up. She listened for a moment, her expression suddenly serious. She motioned her uncle Brock to the phone and handed him the receiver.

"It's the emergency room," Alicia said. "There's been an accident."

"Oh, damn," Brock muttered. His face paled when he spoke to the triage nurse. "I'll be right there. Cassie, Bob, Maria! Ted crashed his truck and the ambulance is on the way to the hospital with him. Hurry!"

Cassie's heart seemed to stop. She couldn't get her feet to move and Brock was yelling at her again to hurry up. Maria was sobbing. Bob had his wife by the arm, guiding her to the car where Brock was waiting impatiently.

"Come on." Bob put his arm around Cassie's shoulder, steering gently to the car, and into the back seat beside Maria.

Brock grabbed the car phone and punched in the hospital number. "Give me the attending surgeon in the E.R. This is Dr. Brock Wellman." He asked a few more questions, then turned to his brother. "Ted swerved to avoid an oncoming car and wrapped his truck around a telephone pole. The other driver called the police on her cell phone and the ambulance got there fast. But we've got to hurry."

Dry-eyed, speechless with shock, Maria reached across the seat and clasped Cassie's hand tightly. Tears flowed down Cassie's cheeks. Why had she been so cold to him? Why, why, couldn't she have controlled her temper and given him credit for all he'd done for her? Ted might die; he might already be dead. And he would never know she loved him—oh, Lord. She hadn't known it herself until this minute. Cassie put her head on Maria's shoulder and sobbed for what never could be. Why did Cassie have to figure out everything too late?

Cassie flung the back door open even before Bob had brought the car to a full stop and ran next to Brock through the automatic emergency room doors. The hospital corridor was a hive of activity. Brock started barking orders at everyone.

"Get me X-rays of his head, ribs, arms, and legs—and get those admission papers here for Cassie to sign. Hook up an IV and start a drip. He's going to need blood so order two units. He's lost a lot from that gash on his arm."

"Cassie, get out of here. Go out in the waiting room with Bob and Maria. Maria shouldn't see this." He guided her through the double-wide swinging doors and shouted more orders. Cassie looked back to catch the briefest glimpse of Ted, unconscious and bloody, lying on a gurney, while the emergency room trauma team came running.

She stumbled forward, right into Bob, who caught her as she fainted.

Cassie came to on the vinyl couch in the waiting room, with most of the Wellman family around her, looking concerned. She fought the fogginess that clouded her mind . . . Maria was crying . . . why?

*Ted!* Her mind seemed to scream. *He had to be dead! He'd died when he'd wrecked his truck and Maria had just found out* . . . Cassie began to sink into darkness again, but a nurse gently patted her cheek.

"Mrs. Wellman. Please try to take a deep breath."

Cassie obeyed numbly, realizing somehow that the nurse meant her when she'd called her Mrs. Wellman. Not Maria.

The nurse and Bob helped her into a chair where she slumped, her head in her hands as she sobbed. Maria put her arms around her shoulders. "Don't cry so hard. You'll make yourself sick, Cassie. The doctors will take care of Ted," she said in a soft voice.

"But Maria, he's already dead," Cassie sobbed harder.

"No, my child. He is not dead and he will not die. He is hurt, but he'll heal."

"I've been so mean to him," she wailed. "I didn't know—"

"I know that you two had a fight, Cassie. When he is well, you can make things right again," Maria said with conviction.

Cassie wondered at her calm demeanor, and then remembered what Maria had been through. Her mother-in-law seemed to have an unshakable faith that God would not take her only living son from her.

Cassie quit crying as abruptly as she had begun. When she felt a little stronger, she got up to pace. Her mood swung from angry to sad every few seconds. One minute she was ready to fall on her knees and beg God for Ted's life. The next minute she was in a fury with herself for being so impatient and self-centered and angry with him all the time. She could barely remember why. None of it was important now.

When she paced down the hall, she saw an image of Ted as she'd seen him in the bus station diner, Ted kissing her as his new bride, Ted nose to nose with her when they'd fought over what his 'real' wife would do and be. When she reached the end of the hall and turned, she envisioned his bruised, broken body in the emergency room and was overwhelmed with feelings she couldn't even name.

Cassie willed him to live, live so that she might have a chance to love him. Life was so hard to understand. And so grotesquely unfair. Despite their differences, she'd seen that they were right for each other in many ways—and she'd hoped they could resolve everything and start over somehow . . .

She rallied against the cold fate that had struck down first John, and now his brother, and wept uncontrollably.

Through her tears, Cassie caught a flash of bright, hot pink—there were bushes blooming by the windows of the hospital corridor. Her granny had called them fire bushes and they were harbingers of spring—the first living things to bring color to the world after winter. Cassie didn't want them to bloom. Her world was suddenly full of death again . . . gray death, like the coldest day of a sunless winter sky.

She went outside for a breath of air and snapped off a blooming sprig of fire bush. She felt like pulling off every single brilliant flower, and . . . Cassie thought again of her grandmother, and how the old woman had cared for those in need. Her granny had had the sense not to argue with God—and the sense to do what needed to be done. She would have known exactly what to do at a time like this.

Cassie thought for a minute more, then went back inside to comfort Maria.

After two more agonizing hours of waiting, Brock pushed open the double doors. "He's going to make it," he said tiredly. "Got a broken right arm and a broken left leg. And one hell of a concussion, plus about sixteen stitches on his forehead." The tears started down his cheeks and his voice broke. "Oh, God. I thought we'd lost him for a while there, Bob." He crossed the waiting room to his brother and hugged him tightly.

"He'll live then." Maria's voice quivered.

"Yes, Maria." Brock stepped back and wiped his eyes. "It'll take a while for him to heal, but he's damned lucky he wasn't killed instantly. Why his air bag never opened is a mystery."

A nurse opened the doors. "Is there a Sassy out here? Mr. Wellman is ready to be moved to intensive care, but he's mumbling about someone named Sassy and he's fighting us."

Cassie dropped the blooming sprig of fire bush she'd held onto. "That's what he called me," she said. "When he didn't know my name he called me Sassy."

"Then come in and hold his hand. Maybe that'll keep him happy."


At exactly eight o'clock the next morning, Ted snapped his eyes wide open, focused somewhat uncertainly on his surroundings, and looked around.

"Momma?" He demanded a full explanation with that one word.

"You're awake," Maria said simply. She went to his bedside just as if it were something she did every morning. She silently gave thanks for answered prayers and kissed him on the forehead.

"What in the hell happened to me?" Ted reached up to feel the bandage on his head. "I remember—sort of. I had a wreck, didn't I?" The memory of swerving to avoid the other car came to him. "Was anyone else injured?"

"No." Cassie wanted to jump for joy, but she kept her voice quiet as the nurses had advised. "They're all fine."

"The lady in the other car managed to pull over," his mother told him. "She wasn't hurt and neither were her kids. But you got pretty banged up."

Ted looked down at his casts and bandages and winced.

"Well, it's nice to see the sun again," he said weakly. "I wasn't sure I was going to. What time is it?"

"Eight in the morning. You've been here since yesterday noon. Cassie and I stayed with you all night." Maria pushed the intercom button on the side of the bed and asked the nurse to page Brock. He came in less than a minute.

"Hello, nephew. You're up bright and early. You must be tougher than I thought." Brock pulled a tiny flashlight from his pocket and looked into both of Ted's eyes. "Hmm," he muttered. "I thought you'd probably come out of that concussion slowly instead of suddenly, but head injuries can be unpredictable."

"I feel like I was the only chicken at a coyote convention." Ted grimaced. "My head hurts like hell, my arm is throbbing, and my leg is killing me."

"Well, thank God." Brock laughed. "Anybody that hurts that bad can't be dead!"


The following days settled into a routine that was painful and boring for Ted; busy from daylight to dark for Cassie.

She was up at five o'clock every morning to help Maria with breakfast and then she was off for a hectic day at work. The minute the clinic closed, she changed from her uniform into jeans and a sweater and rode to the hospital with Brock.

On Tuesday, a week and a half after the accident, Cassie opened the door to his room at exactly five-fifteen. "What's for supper tonight?" she called. "I'm half-starved." Even hospital food tasted fine with Ted around to eat it with.

"Fried chicken." A new nurse answered for Ted. "And Ted seems to have his appetite back. He's going to teach me the two-step when he gets all better."

The nurse fluffed his pillow and accidentally brushed her breast against his arm. Ted didn't seem to notice, even though her thick, flowing dark hair swung past her waist when she bent over him. The nurse had a full mouth, high cheekbones, and Cassie hated her on the spot. Any man would have to be either blind or neutered if he wasn't attracted to this woman.

"Really?" Cassie's tone was noticeably cool.

"Which sister or cousin are you?" the nurse asked impertinently. "I haven't seen a redhaired Wellman yet."

"Oh, I'm a real Wellman, all the same. But I'm not his sister or his cousin."

Cassie crossed the room, threw her arms around Ted, and kissed him on the mouth . . . a long, lingering, wet kiss that surprised both of them.

"I'm his wife," she told the nurse sweetly.

"Well, you devil." The nurse smiled at Ted. I've been

in and out of here all day and you never once mentioned a wife."

"I thought I was getting a divorce come June," Ted said by way of explanation, daring Cassie to deny it.

"Then all's fair in love and war," the nurse said before Cassie could reply. The woman had the nerve to wink at Ted. "Call me when it's over, honey. My name's Charity Lassiter. I'm in the book." She waved to Ted and closed the door.

Cassie turned to Ted, who was pretending to study the acoustical tile on the ceiling.

"Ted . . ." she said meaningfully.

He turned his head on the pillow to look at her.

"Yes?" he said innocently.

"Theodore Ashton Wellman, what's going on here?" she snapped. "How come that nurse thinks she's going dancing with you? You're not going dancing with anyone for a long time."

"Good Lord," Ted said disgustedly. "At least I'm sure she's interested. Before I smashed up my truck you were barely talking to me and now you won't leave me alone. I don't know where I stand with you and I think you like it that way."

He looked at her quizzically.

"Anyway, Cassie, that nurse is just trying to be nice to me. And you."

Poor, innocent Ted, she thought. He didn't even see the potential for a first-class cat fight when he was between the two cats. Cassie had to struggle to keep from laughing. "You know, you could have broken your left arm, Ted." She had to change the subject. "Then I wouldn't have to feed you."

"Maybe Charity could feed me," he retorted.

"I'll do the honors. After all, you're my husband, whether you like the idea or not."

The idea actually made him smile, and Cassie smiled back.

"Ted, I do believe I hear the supper cart coming. Are you as hungry as I am?"

"I sure am. I could eat the north end of a southbound pack mule and have my belt buckle and boots for dessert." His smile turned into a wolfish grin.

"That's pretty hungry," she said.

A chubby nurse's aide brought in two chrome covered trays. Little gold earrings with cowboy boot charms dangled from her earlobes, and for the first time since his accident, Ted remembered what he had on that Sunday.

"Cassie, what happened to my boots and my suit?"

Ted uncovered his tray to find a chicken leg smothered in lumpy white sauce over rice. He put the lid back on.

"Don't even look at this, Cassie. You'll gag. Call the pizza place. We don't have to eat this stuff. Looks like the first person who took a bite didn't like it."

"Now I know you're getting better," she retorted. "You're fussing about your food." She picked up the phone and dialed the now familiar number. "What kind of pizza do you want?"

"Extra cheese. Pepperoni on my half and mushrooms on yours. Tell them to hurry or we'll starve to death, and they'll have to drop our carcasses at the funeral home on the way back." Ted picked up the remote control and turned on the television set.

"Shh." Cassie giggled and placed the order.

"Did you take my suit to the cleaners? Where's my boots?" Ted didn't look at her but concentrated on the quiz show they'd watched together since he'd been in the hospital.

"They cut them off." Cassie propped her feet up and got ready to solve the first quiz before Ted did.

"Cut them off?" he said peevishly. "You let them cut my custom-made boots off? They were handmade—cost me seven hundred dollars. Some wife you are," he fumed. "Did you let them cut off my suit, too?"

"Yes." Cassie tried not to lose her temper over his complaining. Brock had told her that head-injury survivors were often irritable and irrational, and she tried to keep that in mind. "Ted, your suit and shirt were so damaged they couldn't be cleaned or repaired and besides, they were soaked with blood. I told the nurse she could throw them out."

"Damn it, woman, you haven't got a lick of sense," he muttered.

Cassie forgot about the television quiz show and about being hungry. She forgot about the pizza, and everything else, except that she'd spent her evenings in this hospital room with this cranky man for more than a week and he was complaining about a pair of boots and a suit . . . when he had enough money to replace them fifty times. Was it going to be her fault next that he'd wrecked his damn truck?

She did remember to keep her voice low.

"Dead men don't usually care about boots or suits," she said evenly. "No one thought about waiting until you regained consciousness so they could ask you if they could cut off your clothes. They were all too busy trying to save your life. And I come here every damn night trying to save you from dying of boredom—and what thanks do I get?"

Ted reached up to grab her scolding finger and grinned. Damn, Cassie was cute when she was mad. Her hair was curlier than usual and her eyes were sparkling with the effort it took her not to yell.

Every nerve in his body was tingling with excitement. This redhaired hellcat would always make him toe the line—but what a time they would have. She was right, too. Here she'd been waiting on him hand and foot just as if she really did care for him after all, and he'd been taking her for granted.

"I'm sorry, Cassie. You're right. I shouldn't complain. I am most definitely alive—especially when you're around."

"Hmph. Apology not accepted."

"Why not?"

"Because you still haven't told me why that nurse was hanging all over you."

"Hey, I've always been magnetically attractive to women. Wait a minute. No. It only started happening after you came into my life. Guess they know I'm taken, so they want me."

Cassie softened a little. "You're not really taken. We're only married on paper."

"Come here, Cassie," Ted said suddenly. "You know I don't want that nurse. I want you."

"Why?"

He pulled her down to him with his good arm.

"Lie down by me. You need some tender loving care, too."

"Ted, you've got a broken leg and a broken arm. Providing T.L.C. is my job."

"Well, as of tonight, it's my job," he said stubbornly. "Put your head on my shoulder and let someone take care of you for once."

Cassie decided not to argue. She did need some tenderness. She felt like she'd been running herself ragged ever since his accident—running so hard that she didn't know if she was coming or going half the time.

"We need to talk, Cassie."

"What about?"

Ted stroked her hair gently. Cassie felt herself relax a little.

"I care about you, Cassie. I hope you know that."

She nodded, happy to nestle in his arms, although she had no reply at the moment. Cassie had known, in the terrible hours after his accident, that she loved him. Whether or not she wanted to. Whether or not she was married to him. But telling him that *now*—well, that wasn't something she could do just yet.

"And I know you've been here every day since I got hurt to take care of me, and you've been helping Momma out at home, and there's everything else you do for us. I appreciate it. I don't ever want to take you for granted."

"Good," Cassie said. "I'm glad to know you noticed." She pulled out of his embrace for a moment, being extra careful not to jar him in any way, and braced herself on one elbow. Ted stroked her cheek tenderly.

"I've been thinking about a lot of things, Cassie."

"Like what?"

"Like you and me, for starters. This accident might actually be good for me."

"How do you figure that?"

"I almost got killed. I figure I got a second chance at life here. And I don't feel like blowing it."

He was silent for a long moment.

"I guess Momma told you what happened to my brother."

"Yes. She did," Cassie said, very quietly.

"He didn't have a prayer. He never got to—" Ted struggled to speak, and his voice was thick with emotion. "John never got to grow up, or laugh again. Or love anybody. Since he died, I've been stuck . . . in about the same place. I haven't been able to feel anything."

Cassie nodded, and let him talk.

"But that day you walked into my life—" He stopped and looked at her. "Things began to change. Because of you."

Cassie was taken aback. "Oh—"

"Hear me out, Cassie. Up to now we've done more arguing than talking. Or loving. I want to change that."

"I don't think I'm ready, Ted."

"We need to start over. Getting married is no way to begin a relationship." Cassie had to smile.

"I did that to keep you out of the sheriff's clutches. I still don't know why. There was something about you— you looked so lost. And so afraid. Anyway, it's probably the best thing if we do get a divorce or an annulment."

"That was the original plan. I'm not sure I want to change it."

Ted looked at her mournfully, and Cassie almost melted. *Almost.*

"Ted, there are a lot of things I'm not sure about. Exactly how I feel about you . . . I still can't say."

He sighed.

"I know. Look, this is what I'd like to try. We'll still plan on ending the marriage when you turn eighteen, and you'll be safe from Cecil. No matter what, I'll protect you from him. Anyway, until then, let's just try to get to know each other. And ourselves. I've got to deal with my past—my brother's death—" Ted paused. Those were words that might never be easy for him to say, but he went on.

"And you've got to find out who you are, Cassie. And what you want from life. I don't know the answers to those questions. But—"

"But what?"

"I love you. You make me feel like a whole person again. Like I came back to life. I don't ever want to lose you."

"I think I love you, too, but—"

"There are no buts in real love," Ted said stubbornly.

"But there are in real life," Cassie insisted. "I think I should go away after Uncle Ash gets us unhitched. Go back to school and get myself an apartment and grow up some."

Ted frowned. Cassie going away was his worst nightmare at the moment.

"Listen up," she continued, ignoring his mulish expression. "You need some space, too. To find out if I'm the woman you really want."

"I don't need space," he said sulkily. "I need to get these casts off and throw you over my shoulder and take you away and teach you once and for all how much I love you."

"Whoa, cave man. That's not how it's going to be. These are the ground rules: you and I are married in name only. It would probably be better if we didn't even mention the word *marriage* at all if we're really going to get to know each other. And let's try not to drive each other crazy, or bicker too much. Then maybe we can talk about a relationship. But I want a divorce or an annulment first, so we can start over and do it right."

"Okay," he sighed. "Maybe we're both too young to be certain of anything. I guess I have to agree. But I want one concession from you."

"And what might that be?"

"You said you think you love me. Will you give me a chance after we're divorced to show you that I really love you? Then we can talk about—"

Cassie clamped a hand over his mouth.

"Don't say *marriage*, Ted. That's the rule."

# *Chapter Nine*

Ted watched Cassie leave for work with Brock on a fine spring morning near the middle of March, and then he clunked up the stairs to the company's offices over the garage to catch up on the paperwork of his father's business. He pulled open a metal folding chair to prop his casted leg on and spread out a sheaf of government forms on his huge oak desk.

The phone rang.

"Hello. Wellman's," he answered automatically as he thumbed through the new government regulations.

"This here Theodore Wellman?" a strange voice asked.

"Sure is," Ted answered.

"This is Cecil Gorman," the voice said.

Ted damn near dropped the papers. A call from Cassie's cousin was something he hadn't anticipated. "Yes?" he said coldly. "What can I do for you?"

"It's not what you can do for me, it's what I might do for you," Cecil said cryptically. "Give me directions to your office and we'll talk."

"About what?" Ted's voice got even colder.

"As if you didn't know," Cecil sneered. "About Cassie. You don't want me to go to the sheriff's office and get him over there, do you? He'll put Cassie in my truck and she'll be on her way back to San Antone with me faster'n you can say boo."

Ted reluctantly gave him directions and hung up to call his Uncle Ash.

Ten minutes later, Cecil arrived. Ash led him through the living room and up the stairs to the office.

"I only wanted to talk to you, Wellman," Cecil grumbled as he walked across the oak hardwood floor. "Who's this guy?"

Ted looked at him levelly.

Cecil Gorman was a weasel of a man. Not only physically, but in the way his eyes shifted from one part of the room to the other. Ted realized that his visitor was probably sizing up the place and dollar signs were probably ringing up in his avaricious little mind. He wore faded jeans and a faded plaid shirt with cigarette burns just above the pocket on the left side. His teeth were permanently stained from chewing tobacco and there was enough grease in his hair to fry a buzzard. He smelled like he'd walked through some cow pasture somewhere and right up to the business end of a skunk, too.

"Mr. Gorman, this is my Uncle Ash. I've asked him to be present for our conversation. What is it you want to talk about?"

"Cassie." There was an unpleasant look on the little man's face when he said her name.

"Just remember—you're talking about my wife," Ted said warningly.

"I'll get to that," Cecil said. "But hear my story first. My wife 'n' me took her in out of the kindness of our hearts when Granny Stewart died so sudden. We give her a nice room and a decent place to live in exchange for a few chores. And what does she do? Steal from me and run away," he whined.

"What are you getting at?" Ted asked, a lot less patiently.

"I want Cassie to come home." That was a lie, but these two didn't have to know it. Cecil studied Ted's reaction. This boy actually might care for the redheaded baggage. Well, if he wanted Cecil to leave her alone, that was something that could be negotiated. Certainly looked like the Wellman family could afford a little negotiation, unless he missed his guess.

"Why?" Ted asked sharply, never taking his eyes from Cecil's unshaven face.

"My wife is sickly, and we need Cassie's help. We gave her a place to live when the state would've put her in a foster home. But she got lazy and didn't want to work none. The way I was raised, a body had to work to eat, you know. Cassie stole some jewelry and run off, and then the next thing I know the Gainesville sheriff told me you married her. Now just how did you two meet?"

Ted ignored the question, and tried to get Cecil to come to the point.

"Maybe you didn't hear me, Mr. Gorman, what exactly is it you want?

"Like I said, I want the girl." Cecil thrust his stubbly chin up and looked down his nose at Ted.

"Let's talk about her later. You said she stole some stuff. What did she take?"

"My dear, departed aunt's wedding rings, was part of what my grandmother left to me." The awful whine was back.

"How much are they worth?" Ash asked.

"Who knows? She pawned them in San Antone and the pawnshop owner has to keep them for six months before they can be sold. But them rings is still stolen and the law can come down on her for that." He didn't look at the boy.

"Cassie told me they were her mother's rings," Ted said.

"Well, yes. They were," Cecil said reluctantly.

"We seem to be going in circles here. If we could get back to what you want—" Ash said.

"I told you already. I want Cassie back," Cecil said peevishly.

"And if she doesn't want to go?" Ash asked. Whether they liked it or not, this weasel *was* Cassie's legal guardian, and they had to play for time.

"Don't matter a damn what she wants. She's my kin and I'm takin' her. I didn't give my consent for you to marry her, boy," he said angrily to Ted.

Cecil was losing his patience, and these two seemed unable to understand what he was getting at. "I can have your so-called marriage annulled, you know. She's still underage. You just go tell her to get her things together and meet me by my truck. Or else I'm going straight to the sheriff." Cecil jutted out his chin and chanced a look at the young man behind the desk.

"How much?" Ted asked bluntly.

"How much what? Do you mean money?" Cecil laid his grimy hand across his heart and did his best to look offended. "Are you tryin' to buy me off? I figured you'd be tired of her sass by now and glad to get rid of her. You can't actuallly be tellin' me you'd pay me to leave her here."

Ash and Ted exchanged a glance. Now that Cecil had finally gotten around to his real purpose in coming here, maybe they could get rid of him. The sooner, the better, as far as Ted was concerned.

"Now why would I pay you for that?" Ted inquired. "She's not a thing to be bought and sold. Slavery was abolished a few years back, in case you hadn't heard."

"What are you talking about—" Cecil almost got to his feet but Ash pushed him back down into his chair. Ted's voice was less sharp when he spoke again.

"I just want to know how much the rings are worth. I'll pay you back for them. I wouldn't want the whole town to know that I married a common thief. If you go to the sheriff—well, you know how talk gets around in a little town. So let's take care of that problem first. Then we can discuss Cassie. If you need her to come back with you to help your sick wife, then I won't stand in your way."

"Wait a minute." Cecil sounded dismayed. He wasn't going to come away from here with the fat wad of bills he'd expected. Some people might call what he was doing blackmail, but he couldn't call it that if the Wellmans were going to be so cooperative. He hadn't expected them to see things his way. In fact, he'd expected them to want to keep Cassie.

Cecil began again, more slowly, so that there would be no misunderstanding.

"My wife ain't that sick, Mr. Wellman—"

Ted held up a hand to silence him.

"Even so. I think we can help each other out. Now that I know all this about Cassie, I can see that she's going to be trouble with a capital 'T'. She'll probably steal my mother's jewelry next. Hell's bells, why don't you just take her back?"

"Hey—" Cecil tried to get a word in edgewise.

Ted pretended he didn't hear him, and rattled on. "And good luck trying to raise that little hellcat. I've done everything in my power to tame her, but I can't. Yet, Mr. Gorman, you can just tell me what those rings are worth and we'll write you a check right now and you can take Miss Uppity Britches back to Texas."

"Wait. If you two been to bed together, there'll have to be a real divorce." Cecil's bravado was gone and his whine was back again. "But I did hear at the Maysville coffee shop you're not really married to her anyway. You're just saying that so she can hide out here. Is that true, boy?" Cecil narrowed his beady little eyes at Ted. "Are you aidin' and abettin' a teenage runaway? That'll cost you extra."

Ted fought the sudden urge to kick the desk over and skin the man alive, then tack his sorry hide to the smoke-house door. But he forced a polite smile.

"Unfortunately, we really are married. But don't let that stop you. Ash can tell you where she works and you can bring her back to Texas in five minutes. Just tell me what you think those rings are worth."

It was time to get rid of Cecil once and for all, and Ted couldn't wait. Cassie hadn't exaggerated any when she'd told Ted that her cousin Cecil was the lowest, nastiest excuse for a human being on the planet.

"You mean you'd divorce her?" Cecil asked, astonished. Ted had called his bluff.

"Uncle Ash has had the papers drawn up for weeks." Ted nodded towards his uncle.

"I don't believe you," Cecil said flatly.

"Why would I bluff? I had a feeling that she was just using me. She probably wanted to get away from you."

"Hey, I treated her good. I want you to know that. She never wanted for food or anything else—"

"How much?" Ted took a leatherbound checkbook out of the desk drawer and opened it.

"For the rings?" Cecil was dimly aware that these two had gotten the best of him somehow. He couldn't figure out how to retrench, although he'd thought he had this all figured out before he'd driven up to Oklahoma. He'd some interesting plans for the profit he'd expected, too.

He considered Ted's question. These Wellman men looked big and strong, even if one of them had a broken leg at the moment. Granny Stewart had always told Cecil that he was greedy, but not crazy, and he'd considered those words to live by.

He'd never had any intention of taking Cassie back. Legally, he would have no claim to her at all in a few months anyway, and if he went to the sheriff here . . . well, Cassie might have a few stories to tell about him.

Ash noticed Cecil's agitation, and decided it was time to bait the hook. He pulled his billfold from his pocket and removed five twenties. "I'll give you a hundred dollars, Mr. Gorman," he said smoothly.

Cecil didn't need to act offended. He had expected a whole lot more. "My dear, departed aunt's rings was worth a helluva lot more than that!" he said indignantly.

"Five hundred?" Ted picked up a pen.

That sounded a little better. Cecil rolled his eyes heavenward as if asking forgiveness for what he was about to do. "A thousand?" Might as well up the ante, he thought, even though he knew it was an outrageous sum.

"Five hundred and you take Cassie." Ted made out the check and handed it over.

"Hey! No deal! I don't want her!"

"Can we get that in writing?" Ash winked at Ted.

"I'm a little confused here, Mr. Gorman," Ted said. "Do you want Cassie back or not?"

"Hell, no. Do I look stupid?"

Ted bit back a *yes*.

"You'll have to sign a receipt saying that you've been paid the full value of those rings. Cassie owes you nothing now."

Cecil gave him a surly look.

"That good-for-nothin' girl should be paying me back. Not you."

He accepted the proffered check grudgingly.

"What's to keep you from stoppin' payment on this when I leave?" he asked suspiciously.

It took every ounce of willpower in Ted's young body to stay in his chair and not beat the man to death with his crutch.

"As I said, if you accept this check, then Cassie owes you nothing. And my uncle and I both heard you say that you don't want her back. Right?"

"Ye-es," Cecil said slowly, looking from the younger Wellman to the older. He extended a grimy hand to shake on the deal, but Ted nearly broke his knuckles when he shook it.

* * *

Cassie burst through the front door about half an hour later, looking as frightened as a wild doe. She ran smack into Ash, who was just leaving, and almost knocked him down.

"Whoa! Hello, Cassie! Slow down—"

"Oh, Ash," she gasped. "I just saw my cousin's truck in town—Brock gave me a ride home—is Cecil here?"

Ash patted her on the shoulder.

"He was. But we talked him into leaving," Ash said. He wasn't about to steal Ted's thunder. "Go upstairs and Ted will tell you all about it."

"Is he in the office?" she asked.

Ash nodded and she took the stairs two at a time.

Cassie burst in the door.

"Ted?"

He was standing by the window where he'd watched her run into the house.

"I guess you know that Cecil was here. Ash and I got rid of him pretty quick. I doubt that he'll come back."

"What did he want?"

Ted shrugged.

"He didn't want you back, Cassie. He made that clear."

"I was so scared . . ." Cassie crossed the room, put her arms around Ted's neck, and drew his mouth down to hers for a heartfelt kiss.

Ted felt pretty good. In fact, he felt great. He had protected her, just as he told her he would. And now Cecil Gorman was gone . . . forever. He could tell Cassie the details later—just as soon as he got done kissing her back.

# *Chapter Ten*

A few weeks later, Ted's orthopedist pronounced him healed and sawed off the casts. His leg and arm looked pasty white and his skin was peeling where the casts had covered it. Ted got up before the nurse gave him the okay, and he nearly fell.

"It'll be a few days before you walk easily," the orthopedist said. He tested Ted's range of motion and found it acceptable, but gave Ted the name of a physical therapist who could help him strengthen the weakened muscles.

Damn and double damn, Ted thought. The whole time he'd been clomping around in this cast, he'd been dreaming of taking Cassie dancing. Right now he couldn't two-step any faster than an armadillo could fly.

Assisted by the nurse, Ted limped out to the waiting room to pay the final bill, glad the stupid casts were off at last and that he didn't have to dream up ingenious new ways to scratch inside them. He was plagued by the eerie sensation that his healed limbs belonged to somebody else—particularly when he signed the insurance form. His arm and leg just didn't seem to be quite there somehow.

His dad put down the oil trade paper he'd been skimming and rose to help him, but Ted shrugged him off and made it to the parking lot with no help from anything but his late granddaddy's cane.

He climbed in awkwardly, and figured he'd have at least another week or two of limping to look forward to. He *had* planned to get around to cleaning out the room he had shared with his brother for fourteen years. The one that been kept locked, by unspoken agreement. The one that was a vault for the photos of him and his brother that he hadn't wanted to look at, ever again.

Ted had promised himself in the hospital that he would open up that room. But until he could climb stairs—well, it would have to wait. He could amuse himself by making Cassie happy. If she'd let him.

He stared out the window at the passing countryside while his father drove in silence. One thing about the Wellman men—they usually knew when to leave people alone.

Not that sassy Miss Cassie would agree with that, he thought, and smiled just a little. But then she'd been looking more irresistible than ever. And she'd been pretty nice to him since he'd been banged around and broken and turned upside down. Guess she preferred him a little . . . tenderized. If that was the right word.


Another week went by before Ted could manage the stairs at all, and he still had to take his sweet time. One fine day, he decided to go up to the room and get it over with, although no one was home to help him. It was probably just as well.

Momma was out shopping with Maggie for the baby his sister Liz was expecting any day now, and Cassie was . . . somewhere. Probably at work, but she hadn't been there when he'd called, just to say hi and hear her voice. Lord, he was getting attached to her . . . and he was starting not

to mind if she knew it. Cassie would just tell him rudely
not to breathe down her neck all the time, if he broke too
many of her rules. Oh, hell, he thought. She was making
them up as she went along anyway.

Ted started up the seemingly insurmountable stairs.
He'd once taken two at a time without even thinking. But
this particular journey, back to his past could only be taken
one step at a time. He put his foot on the first tread and
pulled himself up. He felt for the worn old key in his
pocket.

From the day Ted had carried his lifeless brother
through the kitchen door he had carried a key in his
pocket. It was worn, although not from use, because he
never used it to open the door of the room that had
been his room, too—until the accident. The key was worn
because Ted used it like a worrying stone, toying with it
when he struggled through something in his mind, until
years of rubbing had made it smooth.

For the first time in seven years he used the key to open
the door. He looked first at the cardboard boxes set on
the beds—boxes full of pictures of him and John.

Two twin beds were separated by a night stand holding
a dusty lamp shaped like a football. Newspaper articles
about calves they'd shown at the county fair, football games
they'd played in junior high, and their favorite pin-up of
a movie star from ten years ago, were all still thumbtacked
to a huge bulletin board on the other side of the room.
A tall chest of drawers and a double dresser sat against
another wall.

He looked again at the two cardboard boxes of pictures.
Pictures of the twins when they had first walked, when they
played T-ball, when Bob first let them drive the tractor . . .
fourteen years of happy life in two cardboard boxes.

Ted picked up the last photo taken of him and John.

The blinds of the room were still drawn, and it was difficult to make out the faces in the faded photopgraph.

He studied it for a moment and put the picture back in the box. It was time to set all of these back where they belonged . . . in the other rooms of the house, where the family lived. He hadn't been able to face these memories for years and his parents hadn't wanted to, either. He looked at the dust on his fingertips and rubbed it off on his jeans. So much dust . . . the dust of the past. It lay thick on every surface in this room.

Ted picked up a baseball bat and took a short swing at an imaginary ball. He set the bat on the bed that had been John's. Last time he'd been in this room his brother had still been very much alive. He wondered what John would have thought of Cassie.

Probably would've thought that Ted was crazy to marry her in the first place and crazier still to agree to divorce her and then try to marry her all over again. But Ted knew his brother would've supported him no matter how things with Cassie had turned out.

"Ted?" A timid voice came through the door. "Is that you in there?"

He nearly jumped out of his skin. *Cassie.* Exactly the person he wanted to see, at exactly the moment he wanted to see her.

He swung open the door and she jumped. "Hi, Cassie. What are you doing home so early?"

"Lord, you scared me. I heard you walking around but I didn't know it was you," she tried to explain. Her heart was pounding from running up the stairs and from the way he'd startled her. "Was this—?" She held back her question.

"This was our room before John died," he said, amazed that he could speak so calmly of his brother's death. "I had Momma move out my stuff the day of the accident and I've never been back. The room had been locked ever since."

"Oh," she said. "Can I come inside?"

"Sure." Ted stepped aside and let her enter. "You can help me take care of something I should have done years ago."

"You were talking about this in the hospital—in a round-about way."

Ted nodded.

"Well, now I'm going to deal with it directly. I guess I'm as ready as I'll ever be."

"Is it ever dusty in here," Cassie said. "I'm surprised Maria hasn't had someone clean up . . . would you like me to do it?"

"Momma never let anyone in here because she thought it would upset me," Ted said. "We all agreed to lock the door and keep it locked. But it's time to open it up. Life has to go on."

Cassie nodded. She didn't know what to say, but she took his hand and gave it a squeeze.

"Cassie . . . you run downstairs and get a dust rag and I'll start sorting through these pictures."

"Okay. I'll change into some jeans and a work shirt and we'll put this room to rights in a hurry."

In a few minutes she was back with a spray can of lemon furniture polish and a handful of clean, white dustrags. "When we finish dusting, I'll vacuum. Open the blinds, Ted. Let's get some light in here."

She put on a pair of jeans so worn they were nearly white, and a T-shirt that had once been pink, but now sported a hole in one sleeve and a paint stain on the other. Her red curls were tied away from her face with a blue bandanna, and she was barefoot. Ted thought she was the most beautiful woman he'd ever seen.

"Brock brought me home early because we were caught up for the first time in weeks. He was on his way to the hospital for rounds," she explained as she dusted. "I thought about reading away the afternoon, but then I heard noises up here and came up to investigate. I'm glad it was only you."

"*Only* me?" he said in mock indignation. "Is that all you think of me?"

She swiped at his nose playfully with the dustrag, and Ted sneezed.

"Bless you!"

"Danks," he said thickly. "Anyway, I'm glad you're here to help me—with all this." He waited for his momentary sniffles to subside, and watched Cassie stretch over the back of the chest to dust. The snug jeans cupped her bottom in a most appealing way, and the vigorous way she cleaned house was energizing him, to say the least.

"That's better," she said when he opened the blinds. "Now I'll start on the nightstands and headboards and you can start sorting the pictures. Good grief, which one is you?" She pointed toward a newspaper clipping, yellowed with age and curling around the edges, tacked to the bulletin board. "I can't tell the difference."

"I'm the one in the blue shirt," Ted laughed. "Momma bought red for John and blue for me all the time. That's how she told us apart."

"But this is a newspaper photo. You're both in black and white." Cassie laughed, too.

"I'm on the one left . . . poetic, huh? I meant to say that I was the left one." He grew serious.

"Yes, you are," Cassie nodded. "And I was the one left when my granny died. But we're alive and we're not alone any more. They wouldn't want us to grieve for them one more day. God knows we've both cried enough."

Ted took her in his arms and held her close for a long moment.

"Thank you, Cassie." His voice was rough with emotion as they clung to each other in the quiet room.

The dust she'd stirred so vigorously danced in the sun that streamed through the windows at last.

"All right," Ted said, kissing her on the forehead. "This feels too good."

"What's wrong with that?" Cassie asked softly, her eyes shining.

"We've got work to do, woman. Don't distract me."

He turned to pick up three pictures and he handed them to her. "These go on the living room mantel. But I'm not able to get up and down the stairs that well."

"I don't mind. Let me do it."

Cassie looked at the top photo. It was a baby picture of the two boys when they were about six months old, both sitting up, both smiling at the camera. Ted wore blue overalls, John wore red.

"You sure were cute little fellows," she said. "Hey! I can tell the difference now. This one is you and this one is John."

Ted looked over her shoulder. "Not even Daddy could tell us apart when we were that young."

"Well, I can," she argued. "This baby one is you. Your eyes are different than John's and your smile is just a little more crooked. Your eyes are softer, Ted."

"I'll be damned," he said, turning the picture over to check the names his mother had jotted on the back. "You're right, Cassie."

"It's easy," she said flippantly, and she dashed down the stairs to put the pictures on the mantel.

"These two hang in the empty spaces in the hallway." Ted handed her two more framed photographs when she returned.

"You tried to fool your mother, didn't you?" Cassie smiled as she studied the pictures. "You and John traded shirts, huh?"

Ted had a choice: faint or fall down. Cassie was amazing. No one had ever known that he and John had traded shirts for their school pictures and neither of them had ever confessed. Every time he and his brother looked at this framed picture they'd been tickled, but no one else had ever gotten the joke. And this family outsider had taken one look and figured it out.

"How'd you know?" Ted asked.

"By your eyes, Ted. I'd know your eyes anywhere."

He stopped picking out pictures and sat down to rest. She picked up her dustrag again and started in on the double dresser.

"So, did you and John always share this room?"

"Yes. Since we were two." He took a very deep breath, and Cassie didn't say anything. She knew he had to come to terms with his past in his own way—and at his own pace. All she could do was help him if he asked.

"Let's keep at it, Cassie," he said quietly. "I promised myself that I would do this and I mean to finish."

She nodded, swiping her dustrag over the top of the dresser until the wood gleamed.

"All dusted," Cassie said with a flip of the rag. "Now I'll chase the vacuum around the room and under the beds. You get some more pictures ready and I'll put them where they belong."

"Yes, ma'am." Ted dug into the box and came up with another two photos. "These go on the end table beside the recliner where Daddy sits."

"All right." She took them and left the room. Seconds later she returned with the vacuum, a noisy beast that Ted had always disliked. And Cassie looked like she meant business. But he didn't think there could be anything prettier than Cassie in a cleaning fit.

"Better stand out in the hall while I do this," she warned him.

"Why?"

"Because if you don't I'll have to ask you to raise your feet and if I vacuum under your feet you'll never get married," Cassie said, without smiling.

"What?"

"Oh, come on." Cassie plugged the machine in the outlet. "You've heard that old superstition. It's not that far from Texas to Oklahoma. Granny always made me go in the other room while she vacuumed."

Ted laughed loudly, but he went to the doorway, where he watched her vacuum up seven years of dust. Never get married? Funny. He was married.

"All done." She wheeled the vacuum back to the hall closet where Maria stored it. "We haven't really made a dent in getting those pictures back. I can carry more than one or two at a time, you know," she said.

"All of these go on top of the piano. But which goes where, Cassie?" he baited her.

Cassie loved this kind of puzzle. She took the pictures and set them out on the bed, trying to figure out how Maria would've arranged them. How had she arranged the ones on the mantel? She put the biggest one in the middle first.

It was a picture of all four kids. Liz was a teenager with a mouthful of braces, Ted and John looked to be about thirteen, and Alicia still had braids. She set a picture of Ted in his blue shirt on the right and an identical one of John in red on the left. Then she picked up the one of Alicia and the two brothers and put it on the other side of Ted, and one of Liz and the two brothers and put it on the other side of John.

"How am I doing?"

"Either you're psychic or you know Momma real well," he said. "Reverse those two on the outside and that's exactly right."

"Damnation, I didn't get it right!" Cassie stamped her foot.

"You were close enough." Ted laughed and swatted at her with a pillow. "You know us better than we know ourselves, Cassie."

She grabbed the pillow and slung it back at him. "It's not hard, Ted. You Wellmans are all so open and kind and easy to—" She stopped herself. She'd almost said *love*. A dangerous word to use, especially here, alone with him and not a soul in the house, and that sexy grin he kept grinning . . . no. She was not going to use that word.

He tried to tease it out of her.

"We're so easy to—what? You didn't finish your sentence, Cassie."

"To—to—clean up after. Now, we've got another whole box of pictures to set out and two beds to change and bedspreads to wash before Maria and Maggie get home," she finished.

"You're a slave driver," he complained. But he could guess what she'd almost said. And knowing that she felt that way made him almost ready to talk about it. About loving her, first and foremost, once and for all.

If Ted could only get her to listen without her being scared to death by the idea that someone might really love her. But the feeling had been growing in him every day since his accident—and he couldn't hold it back forever.

Cassie jumped up and headed out to the hall. "I'm going to get fresh bedding. You can take this dusty old stuff off."

Ted peeled back a bedspread and tossed it on the floor. The cloud of dust that rose made him sneeze all over again, as did Cassie, all the way down the hall and rummaging through the linen closet.

He was hiding behind the door when she returned with two clean bedspreads, and sheets. "Boo!" he said, startling her. Cassie jumped a foot. Then he slapped her rump with a pillow.

"You . . . you . . ." she stammered, her heart beating frantically.

Ted bowed.

"You are challenged, fair maiden, to a duel of pillows. The last hit wins and the winner takes the loser to dinner Friday night."

"Get ready to lose." Cassie grabbed a pillow and whomped him with all her might.

"Oh, no, I will not lose," he declared. "Not to a heartless

hussy like you. I will win and you will pay for dinner at the most expensive place I can think of.'' Ted picked up his pillow and swung low, catching her just below the knees. She tumbled onto the bed but came up with fire in her eyes.

"Think again!" she shouted. She held onto the pillow by the corners and caught him with a solid hit on his good shoulder. He fell onto John's bed but bounded back for more.

She swung at his stomach but missed, the momentum tossing her onto the bed again like a feather in a wind storm. Ted took advantage of her momentary helplessness, and held her knees down with his thigh while he held the pillow above his head with his other hand.

"I win!" he declared.

With a giggle she squirmed out of his arms, took up her pillow, and swung with all her might over his head. He plopped down on the mattress with a thud, spitting out tiny feathers.

"Hah!" she said breathlessly. "That was the last hit."

"Okay, okay. You win. I'll take you to dinner on Friday and you can eat until I'm broke." Ted flipped over on his side and pulled her down beside him. The blue bandanna that had corralled her curls had long since fallen off, and her hair spilled over her shoulders.

"You sure look pretty today." Ted breathed in the intoxicating scent of her. It was a heady mixture of healthy excitement and lemon furniture polish and a trace of sweet perfume.

Cassie giggled.

"Well, thank you very much. I'm not used to getting compliments like that when I clean house."

"I want you to get used to a lifetime of it."

"What—cleaning house?" she said in mock horror.

"No, silly. Compliments."

Ted leaned forward and nuzzled her neck. His mouth touched hers and she closed her eyes, ready for a kiss.

Somewhere down deep a feeling of softness and peace took over his heart. He almost smiled in the middle of the kiss. How could he possibly feel peaceful with a woman like this, he wondered. Cassie, his sweet Cassie, was pure excitement . . . and pure passion, if he was reading her ardent response right.

When he pulled away from the kiss to look into her green eyes, she brought his face down to hers for another kiss that made both of them dizzy. His hand slipped beneath her T-shirt to find her breasts and caress them tenderly. She moaned very softly and shifted her weight, but didn't break the kiss, eager for more of his mouth on hers, and his touch.

A few minutes later her T-shirt was off and she wasn't sure how. Cassie threw it on the floor, then reached around her back and flipped the hooks until her bra was undone. She pitched it on the floor, too, and looked at Ted.

Cassie knew that she loved this man, loved the way he looked at her, loved the passionate yearning in his eyes. Cassie pulled him close, nestling against him a little shyly, but unafraid to return his caresses. Even though she was ready to take this step, she still couldn't control the slight trembling that betrayed her nervousness. She turned away from him suddenly.

"Cassie . . . ?" he questioned, reaching for her hand as she rose. "If you don't want to . . ."

Cassie shut the bedroom door and lay back down beside him on the bed.

"I love you," he murmured. His lips found hers and his hungry hands ran over her breasts and down her sides. "But I want you to want this . . . as much as I do. You can tell me to stop . . ."

"Kiss me again, Ted," she said. "I love you, too."

He drew her into a close embrace, as Cassie began to unbutton his shirt, running her hands over his muscular chest as he deepened the kiss.

Ted was trembling, too, with a barely restrained excitement that coursed through his body—and his soul. Cassie's first time would be his first time, too—and it seemed almost like a dream . . . a beautiful dream that could happen only with the woman he adored. *Cassie*. His true love . . . his one and only . . . his wife.

She arched against him, stroking his chest and back and returning his passionate kisses with an innocent hunger. Ted wanted only to make it wonderful for her, and he unzipped her jeans slowly, touching her as gently as he knew how, until she helped him slide both her jeans and her panties down over her hips and off.

Ted rose from the narrow bed and stood over for a moment, looking at Cassie in all her naked glory, and marveling at the luck that had brought him so lovely a woman—and the love that had kept them together and brought them to this moment.

He quickly shucked the rest of his clothes and stretched his full length along her slender body, sliding his strong hands over her, caressing her all over, until Cassie opened to him, ready and willing to love and be loved. He eased between her thighs, moving gently into her, until she dug her fingernails into his shoulder and drew in a sudden breath. Ted held still then and kissed her forehead, her closed eyes, her lips. He stroked her hair, easing the slight soothing her until the slight pain of her first time eased, and Cassie dreamily opened her eyes.

"Cassie . . . my angel . . . my love . . ."

"Don't stop, Ted," she whispered. "Don't you ever stop loving me this way . . . promise . . ."

He nodded, kissing her lips to seal his promise, and she drew him down to her again.

Ted moved into her with a sensual, tender rhythm, his body hard against her, and she responded eagerly. The fiery sweetness of first love enfolded them both, and the tenderest pleasure she had ever known swept her body. Ted held her and rocked with her, until his own rough cry of release.

"Cassie . . . oh, Cassie . . ."

It was her turn to hold him then, and cradle his head against hers, while she cried just a little, from joy.

He pulled the clean bedspread over both of them and they curled up together, blissfully content in each other's arms, and slept.

They were awakened by the sound of a car door slamming once, then twice.

"That's Momma and Maggie," Ted whispered sleepily. "We better . . ." He yawned.

"We better get up!" Cassie bolted upright. Ted grinned lazily at her.

"Do we have to? This is legal, you know."

She struggled quickly into her work clothes, and tossed his jeans and shirt at him. "Get dressed, lazy!"

He complied, pulling on his clothes carefully. Cassie had made him forget all about his still weak arm and leg, but he was remembering them now. *Ouch. Ow. Oof.*

The front door had opened and closed, and the conversation of the two women who'd come in had stopped. They seemed to be listening. Cassie heard their footsteps on the stairs and Maria calling their names.

"We're up here . . . cleaning," Cassie called back. She blushed. "Lord, we almost got caught," she whispered, glad they'd managed to get their clothing back on and the bed straightened before his mother and aunt made it all the way to the top of the stairs.

Ted grinned wickedly.

"Better do something about your hair." Cassie looked quickly into the mirror. Ted was right. Her red curls were a love-tousled mess. She tied them back fast with the cleanest of the dustrags, and opened the door to Maria and Maggie.

"Uh—hi," she said brightly. "We were just cleaning."

Maria beamed. Maggie smiled. Ted explained.

"Well, we started cleaning, but we got sort of distracted—by a pillow fight," he said hastily. Maria noticed a slight rumple in one bedspread, but she didn't say anything.

"Momma, I tried to uphold the family honor, but I had to let the lady win in the end." He picked up a feather and handed it to Cassie with a flourish and a grin.

Maria saw her son totally reborn in that instant. Her sons' old room had indeed been cleaned until it sparkled. It seemed to her as if the dust of years had been blown away forever, and a fresh breeze came through the open windows, and whispered of spring.

Ted took the key from his pocket and handed it to his mother. "We don't need to lock this room any more, Momma. There are no more ghosts to keep behind closed doors."

"I am so glad." Maria hugged him. "And all the family pictures are back in their places, I see." Tears glistened in her eyes, and she reached down for the corner of an apron she wasn't wearing to wipe them away. "Now both of you take a look at what Maggie and I bought for Liz's new baby when it comes."

The women left the room, and Cassie heard the rustle of shopping bags being emptied onto the kingsized bed in the master bedroom.

"Oh, brother," Ted muttered under his breath. "There's nothing Momma likes more than buying for a layette. How can one tiny baby ever wear so many clothes?"

Cassie gave him a playful swat on his rear, and a surge of pure desire filled her body at just touching him once through the soft denim. Ted turned around with a certain look in his eyes, but Cassie stopped him.

"Oh, no. We're not alone and you just gave your mother the key to that door. You're going to look at baby clothes and you're going to make appreciative noises about each and every itty-bitty nightgown."

She took his hand and pulled him to her. Ted looked

down into her gorgeous green eyes, loving the love he saw there, at last. He held her close for the moment she would allow, relishing the faint smell of lemon furniture polish on the mostly clean dustrag that held back her hair.

*We're going to have an interesting life,* he thought suddenly. And he was finally ready to live it.

# *Chapter Eleven*

Ted spent most of the next day on a tractor, feeling truly healed even though his leg still twinged when he clambered up into the seat. But he didn't let it slow him down any.

He was grimy, sweaty, and whistling when he walked in the back door that evening. "What a wonderful day!" he announced to his father, Maria, and Cassie, who were still sitting at the supper table. "Spring's really here. I can feel it."

Bob nodded. "I've been feeling livelier myself. Remember what that sawbones said, though. You don't want to get too frisky until those weak muscles in your leg heal."

When he said *frisky,* Cassie hid a smile, but Ted saw her dimple up. He grinned.

"I'll try to remember that, Dad. But the physical therapist I've been seeing thought I could handle a little friskiness."

Cassie turned bright red.

Bob nodded again, with a solemnity that belied the twinkle in his eye.

"Sit down, son. We just finished supper, but your mother saved some food for you."

Maria smiled. "I figured you'd be hungry. Working outside builds a hearty appetite."

"Thanks, Momma. I can heat it up in the microwave." He heaped a plate with chicken cutlets, bread and butter, and the solitary ear of corn that was left.

"Think three minutes will heat all this food, Cassie?"

She pushed her chair back.

"Guess I'll have to show you how to push the buttons, huh?"

Bob and Maria didn't look up as she followed their son into the kitchen, but they were hiding smiles of their own.

"Is this the man who's going to live in his great, big cabin in the woods without a woman?" Cassie teased. "You'll have to buy a cookbook. Anyway, it's three minutes for chicken and two minutes for corn. Don't reheat bread for more than thirty seconds or it'll get so hard you can kill a cow with it."

"Okay, okay!" Ted held up both hands in surrender. "I have to learn everything the hard way."

She laughed lightly, a tinkling sound that reminded him of the fancy silver wind chimes his grandparents had sent Momma from south Texas. Cassie only laughed like that when she was really happy, and knowing that made him happy, too.

Ted looked at her sitting at the head of the big kitchen table where Momma made bread and biscuits and cooked for the family. Cassie looked so content that he knew she belonged there ... permanently. He hoped and prayed every day that she would never leave, and he had long since regretted the plan they'd come up with in the hospital room.

Fortunately, they had forgotten to make any rules to cover what happened yesterday in his old room. He hadn't exactly planned it . . . but Ted knew he'd do anything in his power to make it happen again.

Cassie looked at him fondly, realizing that they were hanging around the kitchen just like married folks. Not that she was prepared to make any decisions in that area just yet, no matter what had happened between them the day before. The memory of the searing goodnight kisses they had shared at her bedroom door that same night were enough to make her blush all over again.

Ted noticed the blush and the sparkle in her eyes, and leaned over to give her a long, loving kiss, which made her blush even more.

"Tell me something, Cassie," he said carefully. The microwave interrupted him with an annoying triple beep, and he opened the door to let his food cool. "If you could marry me all over again—if you decide that you want to, that is, after we divorce—what kind of wedding would you like?"

"Oh . . . I don't know," she said impatiently. "I used to dream about an outdoor wedding with my granny sitting in the front row of chairs. I wanted a white satin dress with a long veil and a longer train, and I wanted a big cake and a handsome groom to feed me most of it. But those were just my little girl dreams."

Cassie considered his question for a long moment. "Now I think what I want most is for someone to love me for just me. Not what they think I might be. Not for what they think they could make me into, but just me. I don't know what I want in a wedding, Ted. I don't care about all that foofaraw."

"Well, what do you care about?"

"Finding the right person to spend the rest of my life with. When I'm good and ready to settle down," she answered.

"Give me a hint. What kind of person would that be?"

"A kind and caring man who wants to love me for all

eternity. That's all," she said lightly. This whole subject was making her nervous, anyway.

"That's not the kind of man you want, Cassie." Ted laughed, which annoyed her to no end. "You want someone to keep you on your toes, to keep you guessing about what's just around the corner of life, someone to hold and love you and hang in there and fight with you, too."

"Oh, what would a pigheaded man like you know what a lady wants in a husband?" she retorted.

"Pigs aren't so bad once you get to know them." He laughed again. "They can be right friendly." This was the Cassie he liked best. The spitfire—not the one who sometimes seemed to think her life would turn out like a romance novel. All nice and neatly wrapped up by its happy ending, complete with a tame hero, with muscles between his ears and a ring through his nose.

Cassie just glared at him, stymied for the moment. He had agreed more or less not to talk about marriage, and he had somehow tricked her into doing just that. She wanted to smack him.

She also wanted to throw her arms around his neck and kiss him until he melted like butter on hot biscuits. And she wanted to feel him kiss her back so that warm feeling he caused in her grew until it enveloped her whole body. She wanted to tell him a thousand times that she would *always* love him, but she couldn't. Yesterday had been beautiful for both of them, but in the long run, what if it didn't mean anything at all?

Both of them needed more time to figure out if this was the Real Thing. Or not, as the case may be.

"Hmph," Cassie snorted. "Pigs don't know anything about love. I'm going to bed. I have to get up early. Enjoy your supper. It's stone cold by now and it serves you right."

Cassie ran out of the kitchen and up the stairs. Ted followed right behind her. When they reached her door, he pulled her roughly into his arms and against his broad chest. Then he tilted her chin back and kissed her lightly

on the tip of her nose, her eyelids, and finally on her
closed mouth, until she relented and let him *really* kiss
her.

"Oink, oink," he said when he let her go. He left her
standing there, annoyed all over again, as he ambled
toward his own room.

# Chapter Twelve

Financial records were arranged in neat stacks on the desk in front of Ted. He picked up one stack, rifled through it, shook his head, and set the papers back down. He wondered why he always waited until the last minute to do his personal taxes. Today was April 15, he had to have them in the mail by five o'clock, and he hadn't even begun.

Sun rays danced through the open window, tempting him to come outside. He could almost hear the engine roar in his tractor, or see the trout in the river swimming just under the surface of the water, waiting to be caught. Guy stuff—that's what he wanted to do. Not accountant stuff. Even a good fight with Cassie would be more fun than doing his taxes.

With a heartfelt sigh, Ted picked up a pencil to begin the preliminary report. He filled in his full name, social security number, and started to check the box marked *Single,* when he realized with a start that he would have to file as a married man.

Uncle Sam didn't care how he had been married, or

why. He didn't care if Ted and Cassie had made love only one time. Uncle Sam didn't even care if they never had. They were legally married on December 30 of the previous years as far as the I.R.S. was concerned and to the I.R.S., that meant they had been married all year.

Ted reached across his desk and dialed the clinic. Cassie usually answered the phone first, and she didn't disappoint him this time.

"Cassie?"

"Yes, Ted? Something wrong?"

"I don't think so," he said. "I'm working on my tax return and it just dawned on me that I can't file as single. We were married on December 30, right?"

"Right."

"So as far as Uncle Sam is concerned, we were married all last year." He paused. "Is it all right with you if I file the taxes jointly?" he asked.

"Sure," she said absentmindedly. "Need me to sign anything?"

"Yes. I'll bring the forms down to the clinic when I get finished. Got to get them in the mail by five. Oh, by the way, how about dinner at the Fin and Feather to celebrate getting the taxes done? You don't even have to beat me with a pillow . . . I'll pay. Cassie?"

She set down the receiver with a *thunk,* but he could still hear her voice.

"Good morning, ma'am. We'll be right with you. Please make yourself comfortable and Milly will call you soon," she said, speaking to a patient.

"Was that a yes or a no?" he teased, when she was talking to him again.

"Yes, you exasperating man. Can I go home and change before we go?"

"Of course." His heart was beating faster. "And if you don't take forever primping, we can catch a movie after we eat. What would you like to see?"

"I don't care. So long as it's nothing with blood and

guts. By the way, I don't take forever to get ready to go somewhere," Cassie argued.

"You've never gotten to the church on time. We all have to wait and wait for you," he argued right back. "That's not a good sign, you know."

"Oh, hush," she snapped. "You're not going to trick me into talking about marriage in that roundabout way. See you later when I finish up. I'll starve myself until tonight."

"Are we having a role reversal? Are you going to be the pig tonight?"

"I'm going to hang up on you right now." She hung up.

Ted picked up his financial records and tax forms and started with a newfound sense of purpose. At noon Maria brought up his lunch on a tray.

"Thanks, Momma. Sit down." He picked out a sandwich. "I've got a lot done so I can take a few minutes. You should've seen this desk an hour ago. It looked like a Presidential aide from Washington, D.C., dropped all the paper in the White House on it. I'm making progress, though."

"Doesn't look like it." His mother sat down in the leather chair in front of his desk. "Why are there so many papers for everything we do?"

"I just figured something out, Momma. Because of Cassie, I can file as *Married* this year. That means I get a refund I wouldn't have gotten otherwise . . . about six thousand dollars more."

"Then buy Cassie a used car," Maria said. "If it weren't for her you wouldn't have the money and you don't need it anyway. She shouldn't have to rely on us to take her everywhere she wants to go. I know there are days when I think she'd like to go shopping or just go for a drive, but she's not the kind to impose and ask."

"But—" Ted started.

"But what?" Maria said patiently. "Are you afraid if you

buy her a car she will leave? Give her the freedom she needs. She is still very young, Ted. And perhaps you aren't old enough to understand that when she knows who her heart belongs to . . . and where home is . . . then she'll come back to you."

"I don't want her to leave." Ted stood up and paced. "I love her, Momma, and I'm scared to death of losing her."

"I know. And I know you've loved her for a while. After your accident you two became much closer. But if you love her, you must do what you can to show her. She is afraid, too. Perhaps she is afraid of loving you too much . . ."

"How do you know that?"

Maria smiled. "I was young once, my son, not too long ago. And I am a woman as well as a mother. I know a little about love." She got up and kissed him on the forehead and left, closing the door softly behind her.

In the middle of the afternoon his father wandered in carrying a tall glass of iced tea. "Thought you might be gettin' dry. Doing your taxes is hard work," he laughed.

"Thanks for the refresher. Yeah, this is about as exciting as watching the dust settle in the road when the cars go by." Ted was glad for his father's company. "Actually, I'm almost done. I just have to type the final copy."

"Your mother tells me you'll get a big refund because you're married. She thinks you should buy Cassie a car. I agree with her," Bob said.

"You're both right," Ted nodded. "But if I make it easy for her to leave—well, what if she doesn't come back?"

"Betcha she does." His father's eyes twinkled. "Betcha she's back here in six months. Let's make this interesting."

Ted rolled his eyes and listened.

"I'll bet you one oil well—a producing one—against that ten acres of bottom land with your name on it. If Cassie doesn't come back in six months, you get the oil well. If she does come back, I get the land. If she never

leaves at all, you get the oil well and you get to keep the
land.

Ted groaned.

"Cassie would go up in flames if she thought we were
betting on what she might or might not do."

"Keep it between us, son." Bob winked. "Better get
going. You wouldn't want to keep Cassie waiting for her
special evening out."

"How'd you know what I was planning?"

"I have my ways of finding things out," Bob said affably,
and sauntered out.

If everybody knew so much, why couldn't one smart little
redhead know that he loved her? Ted thought crossly. And
why did she *still* have to argue with him over every little
thing? After the way they'd made love, the way she'd kissed
him afterwards . . . Ted gritted his teeth. Thinking about
making love to Cassie again wasn't going to help him finish
his taxes.

At four o'clock, he was done. Ted cleaned off his desk,
filed everything neatly, and was at the clinic by four-thirty
for Cassie to sign the tax return. She didn't even seem to
look at the figures, didn't seem to care how much her
husband had earned the previous year. She just signed her
married name, Cassie Wellman, as casually as she endorsed
her paychecks, and went back to work.

Ted went to the post office and waited around until a
few minutes past five so he could take her home.

Cassie dashed upstairs to change. For the first time in
weeks, her hair actually cooperated. It went up in a perfect
French twist with springy little tendrils in front of her ears.
She chose a navy knit column dress with a row of tiny gold
buttons from the neck to the slit above her knee, and a
pair of navy high heels with gold ankle straps.

She waited in the living room for him to come down
the stairs. "Well, now, who's waiting for whom? Here I am,
starving to death, and you took forever to get ready. I'm

so hungry the next wind whistling through town could pick me up and blow me all the way to Arkansas."

"Sorry," he said, somewhat insincerely. But the compliment he paid her was heartfelt. "You look absolutely beautiful, Cassie."

He took her in, starting at the fine gold straps that set off her slender ankles and ending at the last curl that had escaped her French twist.

"You don't look so bad yourself." She smiled in a way that made his heart beat faster. "Those jeans seem to have been starched *and* ironed at the cleaners. Are you trying to impress somebody?"

"Come on." He pulled her toward the door. "Before I throw you over my shoulder and have my way with you."

"Cave man," she giggled.

Less than an hour later they were seated at a corner table for two at the Fin and Feather restaurant on the south side of Oklahoma City. A red candle burned brightly in the middle of the table, which was covered with a red checkered cloth. The warm light made Cassie glow even more and Ted wanted her more than ever. The let's-wait-and-see game she was playing was driving him loco.

"Come over here and sit in my lap," he begged suddenly. "I don't care who sees. You look better than anything on this menu."

"I should hope I look better than the chicken and catfish special," she said primly. "Here comes the waitress. Hush." She put a finger over her pouty red lips to hush him properly, and he wished passionately that he could kiss her. Right here, right now.

The waitress was taking Cassie's order, and Ted snapped back to reality.

"Mmm. Well, that entrée sounded good . . . but I'll have the shrimp and chicken dinner . . . and salad with no dressing or tomatoes, and a baked potato with sour cream."

Cassie really was hungry, and she had no intention of

letting Ted's amorous advances get in the way of her supper.

"What would you like, sir?" The waitress turned to Ted and tapped her pencil delicately on her order pad.

"Whatever she just ordered. But I'll have fries instead of a baked potato," Ted said.

The waitress nodded, and headed for the swinging doors that led to the restaurant kitchen.

Cassie hummed a pretty melody somewhat absentmindedly, and looked around the restaurant at the other diners. Not him, Ted noticed.

He seized the opportunity to study her profile in the candlelight. She seemed more beautiful and more—was the word *womanly?*—every day. He listened to her hum, trying to make out the tune.

The smoothness of her voice intrigued him. He could imagine her singing a lullaby . . . it would be a bit off-key, judging from the way he'd heard her sing hymns in church on Sunday, but it would still sound sweet . . .

"Whatever are you thinking about?" she asked. Ted sat up straighter and stopped mooning over her.

"You," he said simply. "I've got good news. I claimed you on our tax return and got back a lot more money than I expected."

"That's nice." She didn't seem particularly interested.

"Cassie, hasn't it ever occurred to you that you could ask for half of everything I own when we get a divorce? You could ask for a settlement, alimony . . ."

"Why would I do that?"

"You're doing it again." Ted shook his head. "You're asking a question instead of answering one."

"I don't want anything you have. Besides, what's half of what a dirt farmer has, anyway? Remember when I thought you were a dirt farmer?" She smiled. "Seriously, Ted, I don't want anything. You've been wonderful to me. You've changed my life. Your family is—I don't think I could find the words to say what they mean to me. I wouldn't do that to you, or them."

Ted considered her words very carefully.

"I can't take anything from you either, Cassie. I would've gotten a refund because I deliberately overpay on my quarterly estimates. But because I was married I got six thousand extra dollars. I—uh—want to buy you a car." Ted spit it out before he could lose his nerve. He'd thought about putting the money in an account for her special use so she could use it for her education if she left him, or just simply giving it to her and letting her do what she wanted with it—but he damned sure hoped she didn't use it to go away forever.

"Nope," she said firmly. "You keep the money. I won't need a car. I can manage. You've done enough."

"I intend to buy you a car or a small pickup." Ted was tired of talking about it and his mind was made up. "You can't talk me out of it," he added just as the waitress brought their food.

"This looks good." Cassie picked up a piece of batter-fried shrimp. "I love shrimp! And I said no. I don't want anything from you. Thanks all the same." She tried to refuse lightly.

His jaw set in that same way it did the night he told her she was too young to know what a wife should do and be.

"You are serious." She looked at him in the candlelight, which cast soft shadows on his handsome face. She had assumed that his family had put him up to this—after all, the Wellmans didn't want for money. But how much had Ted made last year to get a refund for more than she and her grandmother had lived on for a whole year?

"I'm as serious as a heart attack." He wasn't smiling. "Which is what I think you're trying to give me. That amount won't buy a new car but it will buy a decent used one. If you want a new one, say the word and I'll get it for you."

"No," Cassie told him. "I don't even need a used one.

But it would be nice not to have to be so dependent on everyone for rides."

"Then it's done." Ted picked up his knife and cut off a piece of chicken and popped it in his mouth.

"Just like that?" She snapped her fingers. "Ted Wellman, sometimes you make me so damned mad I could spit!"

"What?" He stopped chewing. "I'm buying you a car and you're mad at me? Is there something wrong with this picture, Cassie Wellman?"

"Not a damned thing," she hissed. "Just don't try to buy my loyalty—or whatever you think you're buying—with a car. I can still drive away in it—"

"Yeah?" Ted retorted. "I'm not so sure I'll miss you if you do." His temper flared. "It's your damned money, Cassie. All I'm doing is trying to be decent and give it to you."

She sulked, ate her food without tasting it, and didn't speak to him for ten minutes. *You are a chicken if you don't apologize,* her conscience sing-songed. *You were dead wrong to attack him like that and you know it.*

*I won't,* she argued with herself. *He's pigheaded and hateful to say he won't miss me. When we made love he told me he loved me and now he says he won't miss me if I go, so, I was right. He can't figure out how he feels and neither can I.*

*You're being hateful and your granny would say so herself,* her conscience said. Cassie poked glumly at the last shrimp on her plate, and gave up.

"I'm sorry." Cassie looked across the table at him and knew she'd really hurt his feelings. "I was wrong to be hateful and I'm really sorry. Forgive me?"

"An apology from the Queen of Sass?" His eyes twinkled a little.

"I said I was sorry. What do you want? For me to drop down on my knees and beg?" she said testily.

"That would be a sight to behold." Ted grinned. "Of

course, I'd have to call the undertaker if you did because I've no doubt it would kill you to beg anyone for anything!''

On Monday of the next week a brand new Chevrolet S-10 pickup truck was delivered to Cassie at the clinic. It was candy apple red with red leather interior and the keys were hung on a fourteen carat tag in the shape of a pig. On the back was the inscription: *To Cassie Wellman, the Queen of Sass. From your favorite You-Know-What.*

Cassie had to admit it was magnificent. And she couldn't have needed wheels more at the moment, because Momma had just called with some startling news: Ted's younger sister had decided to get married. Every member of the family had been told to meet at the house, and Momma's parents were flying in from Texas as soon as possible.

# *Chapter Thirteen*

Momma's parents had arrived. No one had expected Momma's grandmother to come with them, but nothing could stop the determined old lady.

She was less than five feet tall, weighed ninety pounds soaking wet, and was at least eighty years old. She spoke fluent Spanish and understood English well, but she rarely spoke it. Her black, long-sleeved dress had a simple white lace collar and the only jewelry she wore was a wide gold wedding band her husband had put on her finger when they wed, and a diamond brooch in the shape of the letter *S* he gave her when they had been married for fifty years.

Everyone called her *Abuelita*. Little Grandmother.

Ted drove to the airport to pick them all up with his father. When Bob helped *Abuelita* from the plane, Ted knew he might have to pick his mother up from a dead faint. His mother's grandmother had been born in Mexico and came across the border to marry the man her parents chose for her when she was fourteen years old. She'd never been outside the state of Texas since except for a few visits with her own people when they were still living.

"Welcome!" Ted hugged his great-grandmother. "We are so glad you have come to visit us." He spoke slowly and clearly so she would understand, but he couldn't keep the excitement from his voice. Then he hugged his grandmother and grandfather. "Momma and Poppa Rhodes, I'm so glad to see you. How did you ever talk *Abuelita* into coming with you?"

"We didn't." Poppa Rhodes shook his head. "She called your grandmother only yesterday and said that she wanted to come to Oklahoma before Liz has her baby. I guess she wants to see the next generation arrive. She also made it clear that she's not going home until Alicia is married properly."

Ted looked at his mother, behind the glass half-wall of the waiting area. She turned pale first, and then squealed and waved like a young teenager.

"Maggie, look who's here!" she yelled, as she crossed the waiting area and hugged her grandmother.

"There is no need to make such a fuss," the elderly woman said patiently, smoothing her black dress, which had been slightly crumpled by Momma's exuberant embrace. 'I am here for the first time, but perhaps it will not be the last."

Maggie had come running and *Abuelita's* dress was creased once more.


A convoy of Wellman family vehicles pulled into the driveway, next to Cassie's new red truck.

"Hello! Welcome!" Cassie waved from the verandah, which she had quickly decorated with huge, colorful paper flowers in honor of *Abuelita*'s unexpected arrival. Ted looked pleased. Cassie had a knack for making things beautiful—without much money.

His sweet Cassie was busy greeting everyone, and she almost seemed to know them all. Ted recollected that she had studied up on family photographs before everyone got there.

Momma Rhodes was a petite and pretty old lady, just as Cassie had expected. Poppa Rhodes wasn't very tall either, but he was muscular from years of hard work. His thick hair had gone mostly gray and his olive-green eyes danced with mischief.

*Abuelita* came slowly up the walk, and shrugged off Ted's assisting arm.

The old woman looked closely at her. "You must be Cassie. You may call me *Abuelita,* as they all do. You have pretty red hair, but your hips look a little small for children. See a good doctor."

She turned back and faced her family.

"Why are you all standing there? Carry my bags into the house, please, Ted. I am tired. I have left my home and traveled in an airplane for the first time, today."

Ted bounded up with several handsome old valises of Spanish leather, incised with bold flower designs that had been painstakingly carved by hand, many years ago.

Cassie helped *Abuelita* with the small bag she carried, and turned to Maria.

"Maria, which room?" Ted had called from the airport to let her know that *Abuelita* had come, but she hadn't had time to prepare a room especially for her.

"The one beside Alicia's. The blue room. If I'd know you were coming, *Abuelita,* I would have a room all fixed up," Maria said respectfully.

"It is not important," the old woman said firmly. "Come with me, my child," she said to Cassie. "Show me this blue room. I want to hear how you and my great-grandson fell in love with each other."

Ted shot Cassie a warning look which she blithely ignored as she took the elderly woman's arm and led her through the back door and up the stairs. "Yes. ma'am," she said. "I'm sure that you want to hear all about it."

Cassie had a feeling that *Abuelita* was a skilled practitioner of the art of matchmaking.

It wasn't long before Cassie was as thick as thieves with Ted's great-grandmother. She was the only one *Abuelita* asked to sit beside her at meal times. Cassie had been requested to help her up the stairs at bedtime and stay with her while the old lady told stories of her childhood in Mexico and the days when she was first married. Cassie was also requested to answer a great many questions about her relationship with Ted.

The old lady confided her cherished dream to Cassie . . . she hoped to see her only great-grandson wed before she died, as well as Alicia. Cassie didn't know quite what to say. She didn't want to dash *Abuelita's* fondest hope— and she didn't want to lead the old lady to believe in something that might not ever happen.

Fortunately, right now the family was absorbed in wedding plans for Alicia—who had unexpectedly chosen the quietest of her swains to bestow her hand upon: Tyler McLaughlin, her college boyfriend, who went around looking like he didn't know *what* had hit him. Cassie was probably the only other outsider who had experienced the Wellmans persuasive talents, and she knew how he felt.

Alicia had recently threatened to elope, throwing the family into a minor uproar, and Cassie prayed that the commotion would take some of the heat off of her, and Ted.

Unfortunately, *Abuelita* seemed determined to see results on all fronts before she went back home to Texas. But so far, she had only managed to talk Maria into throwing an engagement party for her great-granddaughter.

It was nearly midnight, and Alicia's engagement party was nearly over. The band had packed up their instruments and gone home, followed by the catering service staff. The Wellman family had gathered around in the living room to watch Alicia and Tyler open their personal gifts.

Alicia seemed to be happily in charge, and Tyler still looked a little overwhelmed. The happy couple were enthroned on the sofa, with a lapful of presents to open.

The bride-to-be opened cards from her uncles Ash and Brock first, each with several hundred dollars tucked inside. "Wow! Thanks! This is the first month's rent on an apartment when we find one." She waved the money at Tyler, who nodded his thanks.

"No apartments. Open mine." *Abuelita* indicated a big, brown manila envelope.

"What's this?" Alicia opened the envelope and pulled out a thick sheaf of documents. "Looks legal." She passed it all to Tyler, who merely raised an eyebrow.

"This is the deed to the little house your great-grandfather and I started out in. I'm giving it to you so you don't have to live in an apartment." *Abuelita* shuddered politely at the the thought, and Ted winked over the back of the sofa at Cassie.

"It was six acres and five bedrooms, so the children will have a nice play to play," she told them.

Tears filled Alicia's dark eyes as she hugged her great-grandmother. "*Abuelita,* saying thank you is not enough."

"No, it is not, but lots of grandbabies might be." The old lady's dark eyes glittered.

The rest of the family gave the soon-to-be-married pair enough cash and gift certificates to furnish *Abuelita's* "little house" six times over. Alicia wasn't going to need any wedding gifts, Cassie thought. Which was good, because they'd had to talk her into having a formal wedding anyway.

Maria clapped her hands to get everyone's attention.

"'Now it's Cassie's turn!"

"Huh?" Cassie looked at Ted, who wouldn't look at her. "But we're not engaged. We're married. We did it backwards and that doesn't mean we get gifts," she tried to explain.

"But it's your birthday, Cassie," Maria and Maggie chorused. "You've done so much for us—we wanted to do something for you."

Cassie looked over at Ted again, but he was pretending to study an extremely interesting loose thread on the blue velvet upholstery. She'd have to settle his hash later. He knew she hated any kind of fuss.

The family gathered around once more, and Cassie opened generous, thoughtful gifts of cash and jewelry, as if she were in a dream. When she had thanked everyone ten times over, Ted finally decided to look at her.

He handed her a tiny present.

Everyone in the room seemed to have an inkling of just what a present that size might contain, and everyone held their breath.

It was wrapped in bright red, shiny paper and had a gold bow on top. There was a card not much bigger than a postage stamp hanging from the bow. She opened it and read a very simple message . . . *With Love. Ted.*

Cassie was dismayed, but didn't want to show it. It had to be a ring. But surely Ted had enough tact not to embarrass her with an engagement diamond that she wasn't ready for in front of them all.

She took off the red, shiny paper, and bow to reveal a gold foil box. She took the lid off, expecting to find a jeweler's box inside. She wasn't disappointed. There it was . . . in red velvet, no less.

Cassie flipped the lid, realized what was inside, and yelled loud enough to raise the roof. She threw her arms around his neck and kissed him all over his face, as tears streamed down her cheeks.

"What is it?" Alicia knew it had to be a huge diamond to get that kind of reaction.

"Must be a chunk of ice as big as my foot to make her holler like that," Brock chuckled. "I've never seen her look so happy. Not even on the day they delivered her new truck to the clinic. Come on, Cassie. Are you going to show us what's in the box or not?''

She didn't seem to hear his question.

"Ted—you're an angel. You are a perfect sweetheart. How did you ever find them?"

Everyone's curiosity was piqued, and they craned their necks to see.

Ted's face was as red as a boiled lobster. He hadn't known exactly how she'd react to his gift, and at the last moment he'd been afraid she'd be disappointed.

But holy smoke and damnation, they'd more or less promised each other not to mention anything to do with marriage, and Ted wasn't about to give her an engagement ring of her own until he was absolutely sure that was what she wanted.

"What did Ted give you, Cassie?" *Abuelita* asked inquisitively.

"Look." Cassie perched on Ted's knee and turned the box around to show them a tiny little engagement ring and a plain gold band that matched. The rings were old-fashioned in style, and it suddenly dawned on Maria why they had meant so much to Cassie.

"They're my mother's rings," Cassie said proudly. "The very same ones I sold to buy a bus ticket when I ran away. They're the only thing I had of my mother's. And Ted has bought them back for me!"

Late that night, in the wee hours of the morning, Ted laced his hands behind his neck and sighed again, for the hundredth time. He'd made Cassie happy—truly happy— and that made him feel remarkably good. He was thinking about the way she'd kissed him for his simple gift when he heard a faint knock on the door.

"Come in," he said softly, not really so very surprised

to see her sneak in the door and cross the room to his bed.

"Ted, I can't sleep," she whispered.

"I can't either."

He rolled over in his bed and propped himself up on one elbow. Even in the dim glow from hall light, Cassie could see that he was barechested. The covers were drawn up only to his waist.

"Come here, Cassie."

The look in his dark eyes dared her to say no. She didn't.

Cassie locked the door with a faint but definite *click*. She raised her nightshirt over her head, revealing nothing but milky skin underneath.

Ted couldn't help but feast his eyes upon her. She was as beautiful as any goddess in her nakedness, and he pulled her under the covers with him, and ran his hands over her body. Her mouth sought his, demanding kisses . . . and more.

"God almighty," he gasped. "Cassie, you are so beautiful. I love you so much. Don't ever leave me. I'd do anything to keep you . . ."

"Shh." She put her fingers over his mouth. "We don't need to talk about that now. Make love to me Ted. The way you did the first time. I want you—*now.*"

This time he didn't fumble. His natural tenderness and his sincere love for the woman by his side lent him patience when she wanted to forge ahead with the experience . . . made him know instinctively just how to touch her in all the places that made her beg for more . . . and finally drove him to make wild, fervent love with her until those same crazy fireworks lit up the world for both of them.

Ted held her close afterward for the longest time, until she opened her eyes to see him stretched full length in a sensual languor with an indescribable smile on his face. Cassie was so weak with pleasure she could barely move, except to caress him with a touch as soft as the darkness that surrounded them.

"Oh, Ted. That was . . . wonderful."

"Mmmm," he agreed sleepily.

"Would you mind . . . if we start all over again?" she whispered into his ear, gently nibbling the lobe.

"Why, Cassie . . . that's exactly what I had in mind," he whispered back. He nuzzled her throat and his kisses moved down her body until he had lit a fire deep within her . . . and they were consumed together.

# *Chapter Fourteen*

The next Sunday Liz went into labor. *Abuelita* had come to visit, to discuss baby names, and to give her the baby clothes she had knitted. Suddenly, Liz's water broke, flooding the chair, the floor, and as Liz said later, erasing the last vestiges of dignity she had.

Brock drove her and her husband to the hospital and the rest of the family straggled into the waiting room a few at a time through the afternoon to await the arrival of the next generation.

It was a memorable experience as far as Cassie was concerned. She looked around at everyone and wondered if all families went *en masse* to the hospital when a new baby was about to be born. Would they all be waiting like this some day for her to deliver? She blushed at her thoughts . . . and the memory of making love with Ted.

She knew where babies came from, and what birth control was for, and she simply hadn't bothered. Cassie shifted nervously. She could be where Liz was right now in about eight months. She passed the time by mentally calculating the days of her cycle, and decided not to worry too much.

They'd managed to make love on her "safe" days, through sheer dumb luck.

But what on earth would she do if their lovemaking brought a baby into the picture? She'd feel obligated to stay married to Ted then, and he'd feel trapped. They'd have to be more responsible next time . . .

Before Cassie could think about it anymore, Liz's husband Daniel burst through the waiting room doors. A blue paper mask dangled around his neck and he wore a disposable scrub suit to match. "It's a girl!" he yelled joyfully. "And it looks like she has my mother's red hair. Cassie, you won't be the only redheaded Wellman after all!"

"Look, Ted," Cassie stood in awe in front of the nursery window, watching the nurses give the tiny baby a sponge bath. "Look at her little ears and toes. Oh . . . look at all that red hair."

"Guess you jinxed her," he whispered as he, too, looked on in wonder at his newborn niece's miniature perfection. He put his arms around Cassie's waist from behind. "We're her aunt and uncle. How do you like that?"

"I like it very much," she said simply. Ted turned her around to kiss her before the nurses looked up.

In two days Liz brought the baby to her mother's house. And in almost no time that little human being had wrapped Cassie firmly around her tiniest finger. During the week, if Ted wanted to find his wife, all he had to do was to go to the nursery Maria had set up just off the living room on the first floor of the house. When Cassie wasn't at work, she and *Abuelita* were in the nursery, usually just watching little Rose.

The night Liz and her husband took the baby home, Cassie paced the living room floor restlessly. She picked up a magazine and tossed it aside. She tried to watch sitcoms on television but the jokes didn't make sense and her mind wandered. She thought about driving her truck into town and sitting at the Dairy Dip with a soda for a while, just to watch the people come and go, but that didn't tempt her either. Evidently she was in one of her Jesus moods, as her granny used to call them. Granny had said that Cassie didn't know what she wanted, wouldn't want it if she got it and Jesus himself couldn't live with her.

She put on a pair of cut-off blue jeans and Ted's T-shirt, which was still several sizes too big, and went out to sit on the porch swing. Maybe some time alone would be good . . . she'd work this restlessness out of her mind while the frogs chirped and the swing creaked. But the night was too hot for frogs, and the swing had been oiled since she'd last swung in it.

"Hi." Ted came around unexpectedly from the back of the house. "Supper's over already?" He was filthy. His boots were caked with mud and his once-white T-shirt looked like it had been fished up from the bottom of Blue River. The dust in his hair made it look brown instead of black and a fine rim of dirt lined his forehead where his hat had been.

"You've been working hard," she said, without emotion.

"Yep, and I'm hungry as a bear. Let me shuck these dirty clothes and take a shower. Maybe I'll bring my plate out here and eat on the front porch." He disappeared before Cassie could tell him that nobody, and she meant nobody who still needed to breathe to live, wanted to be in the same county with her when she was in a mood like this.

She finally sorted through her feelings long enough to realize that this mood had settled in when Liz and Daniel took baby Rose home. But it wasn't as if Rose was her baby, no matter how much she missed her . . . what was really wrong with her?

Ted backed out of the door, carrying his supper on a

tray. "Got room for a passenger?" he asked and sat down beside Cassie before she could answer. The swing stopped as he began to eat and her mood worsened.

"I'd like to show you something when I finish eating," he said. He shoveled in the food, which annoyed her more than a little. "Okay with you?"

She started to snap at him and tell him she didn't give a damn. But something inside her heart told her he didn't even know she was angry. Really, no man should have to put up with a moody witch like her.

"Not very talkative tonight, are you?" Ted popped a chunk of buttered biscuit into his mouth.

Cassie shook her head.

"Missing Miss Rose?"

"Yep," she answered.

He looked at her for a moment. "Is this the first time you've ever been around a tiny baby?" he asked curiously.

"Yep," she said again.

"Hey, if you want to be alone, just say so. I know how you feel. There's been times when I damn sure didn't want to be talked to. After John died there were times I thought I would scream when people talked to me." Ted cocked his head to one side and studied her.

"I think I would like to be alone," she said, wondering if her black mood would get her into another pointless fight.

He picked up his tray and kissed her lightly on the forehead. "I still want to show you something later if you want. If not, you can see it another time. Come and get me if you want company." Ted crossed the porch, and went back into the house.

His family would probably think they'd been fighting again, she thought, but they hadn't for a while. He seemed to be changing in ways that she liked, whether he knew it or not.

Cassie wished she could say the same for herself. She'd been slipping into a funk ever since little Miss Rose had been born. But Cassie could see Miss Rose every day if she wanted. Liz was sweet and understanding, and she welcomed her help with the baby.

Her granny would have said flatly that Cassie was getting broody—wanted a baby of her own. She squelched the thought. She was only eighteen years old and she wanted to go back to school, not have a baby. She wanted to get started on a real career—and a real life.

Sure. Right. Whatever that was.

# *Chapter Fifteen*

Ted finished his supper in the kitchen, quietly climbed the stairs to his bedroom, flopped down on the bed and tried to make some sense of this dull ache in his heart. He had an awful feeling that Cassie was getting ready to run away again. She'd been in a terrible mood all day . . . now she wouldn't talk to him. Something was up, he just knew it. If she wanted to go, he couldn't keep her. She was young, just barely eighteen . . . but then Alicia was only a little older, and she was ready to settle down. He was twenty-one . . . just one year younger than Tyler, his sister's fiancé. It wasn't uncommon for a girl to get married right out of high school and it wasn't uncommon for a man his age to accept the responsibility of a wife and family. But if she wanted her freedom, he loved her enough to let her go. Even if it half-killed him.

There was a gentle knock on his door.

"Yes?" he answered without taking his eyes from the spot on the ceiling where he'd swatted a fly several months ago.

"Can I come in?" Cassie opened the door just slightly.

"Sure."

"I'd like to see what it is you wanted to show me, but if you're tired . . ."

"Come sit beside me." Ted patted the edge of the bed.

She left the door open and sat on the edge of the bed. He took her small hand in his big one. "Are you in a better mood?"

"Yep," she nodded.

"What's so funny?" Her impish grin was back and so was the twinkle in the green eyes that had been almost lifeless half an hour before.

"I get in these moods sometimes," she said. "Granny called them my Jesus moods. I'm pretty hard to live with when I'm in the middle of one. She said I didn't know what I wanted, and wouldn't want it if I got it, and Jesus himself couldn't live with me then."

"I'll try to remember that in the future." He gave her hand a warm squeeze. "I guess I don't stand a chance if the man from Galilee couldn't live with you."

"What did you want to show me? The inside of your bedroom? I've seen it," she teased.

"You sassy piece of baggage." Ted grabbed her and pulled her down beside him, giving her a quick kiss.

She didn't push him away.

"No, I don't want to show you my bedroom." He rolled off the other side of the bed and picked up his sneakers. "You still wearing those sandals you had on out on the porch?"

"Yep." She raised one shapely leg and shook it at him.

"Then go put on some sneakers and socks. We're going to take a long walk and it could be past midnight when we get back." Ted tugged his shoes on and took a T-shirt from the drawer of a massive chest.

"Okay," she agreed. "I'll be downstairs in five minutes. Betcha I beat you."

They met at the top of the stairs in two minutes, both of them out of breath and giggling. Bob and Maria were sitting in the living room, watching television, and although one of them winked, they acted pretty much as if Ted and Cassie weren't even in the house, let alone flirting with each other.

"Be back later," Ted yelled over his shoulder as they dashed through the living room and out the back door.

Once they were safely outside, Ted took Cassie's hand and paced his steps to hers. "We could drive the first mile in the truck, but it's a nice night. Let's see if we can talk for a whole mile without fighting."

"Hmm," she murmured. "We don't have enough neutral topics to walk a whole mile without bickering."

"Let's start with Rose then," he said off the top of his head.

"Oh, Ted, isn't she the most adorable little thing you've ever seen? I was honored when they named her Rose after my middle name." Ted smiled down at her. The stars threw off less light than she did right then.

"It is a pretty name," he agreed.

"Must be something words can't describe to know your love produces something like Miss Rose," Cassie added.

"Sometimes babies get produced when there is no love," Ted said honestly.

"No," she disagreed. "Babies get made and born every minute, but it takes love to make a baby like Rose."

They walked in silence for a while, breathing in the hot night air and listening to the crickets' serenade. The black dirt was packed hard under their feet and weeds grew in the ruts where Ted's old work truck drove back and forth several times a day. Finally, to avoid bumping into one another, Ted walked in one rut and Cassie walked in the other, and they held hands across the weedy middle.

"Well, we've come at least a quarter of a mile and you haven't bitten my head off yet. Do you think it's the heat? Maybe we're only going to fight when it's cold," he said.

"Maybe you're right." She surprised herself by agreeing. It had been on the tip of her tongue to lash out at him, to remind him she only bit his head off when he was being obstinate.

"So how much longer do we have to be angels? How far is it to this something you want to show me?"

He grinned. "About a half a mile to the end of this road, then about half a mile back down the lane."

"Another mile? Do you expect me to keep my halo straight?" she asked. "That's tough for a redhead. Maybe I'd be less argumentative if I dyed my hair."

"Don't. I like it red."

"Careful. We're on the verge of an argument."

"Is this an argument?"

"No. It's a reasonable discussion. Can't you tell the difference?"

"Cassie—" he said warningly.

"Is this the lane you're talkin' about?" Cassie conveniently changed the subject.

"Yes," he nodded. "It leads right down to the surprise. I was going to wait until it was finished to show it to you, but I couldn't. I want to share it with you right now."

After a while she could see the form of something in the moonlight, rising up at the end of the long path. It looked like the skeleton of a house, one that was falling down from years of neglect. After a few hundred feet more, she could see plainly it wasn't an old house, but a new one in the first stages of building.

"Ta-da! My surprise. You're the first to see it." Ted let go of her hand and with a wide sweep introduced her to the house. "I've hired a crew to help me frame it up. It's more work than I thought. Guess I got carried away."

"It's beautiful," she whispered, awestruck by the sheer size of the two-storey house, nestled down in a glade surrounded by trees.

"Dad said there was a house here once, but it burned down years and years ago. The trees were small then, but since no one was interested in building way back in here again, the forest grew back. I love the quietness, don't you?" He took her hand again. "I want you to come inside and let me show you around. Do you like the big verandah?"

He indicated a wraparound porch that existed only in his mind's eye. "I could hang a porch swing over there at that end and put a split rail fence all around. This is the front door. Come right inside, Cassie." Ted pulled her through the two-by-four studs where a door would be hung in the future.

"Oh, it's just lovely. It looks like the "Before" pictures in *Better Homes and Gardens,*" she giggled.

"Don't make fun," he said in mock seriousness. "When this house is finished it could be featured in that magazine." He pointed out more imaginary features. "This is where the fireplace will be, and there will be glass doors covering the bookcases on each side that go from floor to ceiling." He didn't tell her that the bookcases were especially for her since she liked to read so much.

"I can't even imagine owning that many books," she whispered.

"This is the kitchen." He took her through another set of studs. "Which will have all the modern-day conveniences. How does that strike you?"

"You are up-to-date," she agreed, laughing. "What's your color scheme?"

"Hadn't made up my mind yet. What do you think would look good in a log house in the woods?" he asked.

"Blue," she said without hesitation. "The same blue as the sky in the winter. With touches of green here and there and maybe a little mauve to pick up the summer sunset. A house in a natural setting should have natural colors. It's going to be lovely." Cassie turned around and in a moment could visualize the whole kitchen . . . could almost smell cookies baking in the oven, almost hear little Rose laughing as she swung on the porch swing, and waited to eat some.

"Okay," Ted moved on. "Want to see the bedrooms?"

"Why, Ted Wellman!" she exclaimed. "Here we are in the middle of nowhere and you want to take me to the bedroom . . ."

"Don't tempt me, woman," he chuckled. "Now, the master bedroom is back here. Those holes in the floor are where the plumbing goes in for the master bathroom. There'll be a garden tub, a big glassed-in shower stall and a powder room. The other three bedrooms are upstairs with doors that open onto the upstairs porch."

"Why such a big house for an old bachelor who can't even remember how long to microwave his supper?" she asked bluntly.

His tongue was suddenly glued to the roof of his mouth. He felt the way he had on his first day of school and the teacher asked him his name. "Cassie," he finally cleared his throat and spoke. "I've always wanted to build this house. But I never expected to live in it all alone. I was hoping you'd want to share it with me—someday."

Tears came to her eyes. She jerked her hand free of his and stumbled through the studs back to the front porch.

Ted followed her. "I'm asking you to be my wife and not just on paper. I'm asking you to marry me because I know in my heart I love you and I don't want to live without you," he said honestly. But Cassie didn't seem to want to listen.

"It isn't real, Ted."

"I know what I feel for you, Cassie. It's sure as hell real."

"Ted, I have to know beyond a shadow of a doubt that you love me . . . not just for the moment . . . not just for what we do when we fall into bed together. I have to know that you want to stay with me forever." The words were from the bottom of Cassie's heart and it hurt her soul to say them.

"I can promise you that I will. And I love you and if you love me, that should be the end of it." Ted put his arm around her shoulders, but she pulled away.

"You haven't known any woman but me," she argued.

"Oh, Cassie . . . what do you feel when I kiss you? When we make love with each other? Do you feel like the world explodes into fireworks? Do you feel like your insides are turning into mush and there's not a damn thing you can do about it? Do you want the kiss to go on forever and ever and never end? Do you want to melt in my arms and stay there for all eternity?" He turned her around to face him, tilted her delicate chin up until she could see nothing but his soft brown eyes, made even softer by the light of the moon, and kissed her. A kiss that lasted several minutes and melted her insides to mush.

"Ted," she murmured. Her better judgment had turned to mush as well.

"No," he said. "I want you so bad it hurts, but not tonight. Not here. If we make love in this house it's going to be when you've told me you'll be my wife forever."

# Chapter Sixteen

The wedding was planned for two o'clock in the afternoon. A huge white arch covered with ribbons, twining ivy, and roses stood under the shade of tall pecan trees. The bride and groom were to leave the reception by limousine to be driven to the Oklahoma City airport for a midnight flight to the Bahamas. The newlyweds planned to honeymoon at a secluded resort on the remote side of the island. Alicia was ecstatic, and Tyler still hadn't said much. And he still looked like he didn't know what'd hit him.

Cassie woke at five that morning after a sleepless night. Tomorrow she would pack her suitcases and drive away in the candy apple red truck. Right to Ash's office to sign her divorce papers and then she would go back to Texas, and back to college.

She kicked off the covers and opened the drapes. The leafy trees rustled in the warm breeze, displaying several shades of green. They'd been bare the first time Alicia opened the drapes for her seven months ago. Like the love she had for this family, they had budded and grown. She wondered what she would do if Ted never came to get her . . . if he found out he wasn't in love with her after all.

"Cassie!" Alicia burst into the room without knocking. "Today is the day and I'm so nervous I'm about to puke! What if Tyler doesn't show up? I can't see him all day and what if he changes his mind? Cassie, what if my hair won't fit in a circlet of rose buds?"

"You've got a case of the jitters and you've got 'em bad," Cassie laughed.

Alicia rolled her eyes.

"I haven't slept a wink since Tyler kissed me at five minutes till mdnight. Now I wish I'd made love to him every night for the last week so I'd know he would come back for more! Damn it all, we should have eloped!"

'You'll do fine," Cassie said firmly. "Let's go grab a sweet roll and get you some milk to calm your stomach. Then we'll watch Saturday morning cartoons until Liz gets here to do our hair."

At seven-thirty Liz arrived with a bushel basket of hot curlers, hair spray, mousse, and make-up. "Cartoons?" She raised one eyebrow and laughed. "That's the joy of a Saturday afternoon wedding. Of course, a Saturday morning wedding gives you less time to think about it and get sick to your stomach. Guess what Tyler is doing right now."

"Have you seen him?" Alicia's eyes glittered. "Momma says I can't even call him on the phone. I can't see him and I can't talk to him until we say our vows. Isn't that stupid. Liz, I swear we should have eloped."

"Oh, no," *Abuelita* brought a cup of coffee from the kitchen. "You are doing this right. No great-granddaughter of mine is going to elope. This is the best day of your life. It's the only day of your life you can take all day to get dressed."

"*Abuelita*, what if Tyler falls out of love with me?" Alicia sat beside her great-grandmother and rested her head on the elderly woman's shoulder. "How did you know you were doing the right thing when you married?"

*Abuelita* set the cup down on the end table and patted her granddaughter on the arm. "Why do you young woman doubt your hearts? You worry your mind about matters your heart would not question. Today Tyler loves you. Make today the most important day of your life, and tomorrow will take care of itself. Now go upstairs and become a beautiful bride for Tyler, and let this old woman drink her coffee in peace."

"I love you," Alicia kissed her on the cheek. "And you'll never be old, so quit saying that."

*Abuelita* smiled but she didn't argue. She hoped Cassie heard the advice she'd given her great-granddaughter. The words had been meant for her as well.

Thirty minutes before the wedding, Cassie and Liz fluffed up the white Chantilly lace dress and put it on Alicia. They slid it over her head, buttoned the thirty-six covered buttons up the back and the six on each pointed sleeve, then turned her around to see herself in the floor-length mirror.

"Is that really me?" Alicia squealed. "Liz, my hair is gorgeous. Where were you all those mornings when I was trying to fix it for school?"

"Having morning sickness," Liz said wryly.

"You are beautiful." Cassie kissed Alicia gently on the cheek. "Just incredibly beautiful—like every happy bride."

There was a soft knock on the door and Bob pushed it open. "I hear I've got a daughter in here. Cassie, where is she? Who is this ravishing bride? Surely this can't be Alicia?"

"Oh, Daddy, I love you." Alicia swept over and kissed him on the cheek.

"Tyler's waiting for his cue to follow the preacher out the front door . . . wait, I hear the music now. He's asked the most foolish questions today. Most I ever heard him say. He even asked me what he would do if you decided you didn't love him." Bob smiled.

"Did he really?" Alicia's eyes widened. "But I'll always love him."

"Of course you will. That's what I told him anyway. Now there's my cue to get you girls to the living room and start the procession. Let's go. Tyler'll faint if he has to stand up there very long." Bob crooked his elbow and offered it to his daughter.


Bob and Alicia paused on the porch. Her dress, an exact replica of Maria's wedding dress, was white bridal satin covered with Chantilly lace. The skirt fell from a basque waist, topped with a bodice with a Victorian neckline. The sleeves extended into points that covered the tops of her hands. The bottom of the dress was scalloped and fell just above her ankles, showing off high-heeled kid leather bridal boots. Her illusion veil fell from a circlet of white roses which gleamed in her black hair.

Ted thought his sister was a lovely bride. But neither she, nor any other woman there, could outshine Cassie in his eyes. She couldn't be more beautiful than she was right at that moment. All the love that was in his heart was visible in his eyes, and it made Cassie uncomfortable. She looked at him and had to look away.

The preacher got through the preliminaries without Ted even hearing. Cassie sneaked another look at him and he winked. She blushed.

"In Corinthians, we read that love is patient, love is kind, love does not want its own way . . . "the good man droned on, as Cassie smiled back at Ted, and thought of all the times they had done exactly the opposite.

"Who gives this woman to be married to this man?" the preacher asked finally.

"Her mother and I do," Bob said clearly, then sat down in the front row beside Maria, taking her hand firmly in his.

Cassie swallowed a lump in her throat, and tried to will

the lump in her heart away. She might have a wedding someday. If Ted was honest with her and with himself, it might be possible to marry him. But there would never be a father to give her away and never a mother to sit beside.

She chided herself for giving in to self-pity. *Bob would gladly walk you down the aisle,* she told herself. *Or he'd walk Ted down the aisle to you and say he'd give Ted to be your husband. Hasn't Ted said you always have to do things your way?* Cassie couldn't control the smile at the corners of her mouth.

The wedding continued but her thoughts were elsewhere. Had Ted just mouthed the words *Marry me* behind the preacher's back? Almost imperceptibly, Cassie shook her head.

The newlyweds led the first dance, and soon everyone was out on the floor. Except Ted and Cassie. He got a good grip on her and marched her over to his great-grandmother. *"Abuelita,* help me. Cassie's going away. Can you talk some sense into her head?"

Cassie shook her head. "In a few days you'll be glad I didn't say yes. You've caught a marriage virus, that's all."

"What more can I say?" *Abuelita* fiddled with the rings on her fingers. "I have talked until I am blue in the face, and that's a lot of talk for a Mexican grandmother who is as brown as I am! Cassie is as stubborn as a mule. She does not listen to a wise old woman. She does not listen to her handsome man whose eyes are filled with love. She has to go away to prove something to herself, but it won't take her long to prove it. However, I don't think she is completely foolish. Now go and dance this slow dance. Maybe if you hold her tight . . ."

Cassie had to laugh.

"Is she right?" Ted asked when they were dancing.

"Just hold me and don't talk," she said. "I honestly don't know the answer."

# *Chapter Seventeen*

The battle started when Cassie went to bed that morning at two o'clock. The bride and groom had long since boarded their flight, the band had gone home, and so had the last reception guests. The kitchen looked like a Texas twister and a hurricane had met in the middle of it, but Maria said hired help would take care of it tomorrow. Ted walked Cassie to her door and kissed her gently on the cheek. He didn't ask her to reconsider, but he didn't say goodbye either.

Cassie Stewart O'Malley Wellman took off her gorgeous mint green satin dress and draped it over the back of a chair. She threw her pantyhose on the floor beside the matching satin shoes and took all the pins from her hair, letting it fall in natural ringlets to her shoulders. She soaked for an hour in the tub, realizing that this would be the last time the bedroom and bathroom were hers. In a few hours she would have her maiden name back and her freedom.

She dried herself quickly and put on the same nightshirt Alicia had brought her the first day she came here. Every-

thing else was packed and ready to load in the morning
. . . after she said the good-byes she dreaded to the family.
She turned out the lights and fell into bed. It was going
to be easier than she thought. She'd be asleep in seconds,
exhausted as she was, and after a few tearful good-byes
tomorrow morning, it would all be over. And Ted could
start to date other women . . .

Her conscience reminded her that she was only eighteen
years old and that she had a whole life ahead of her. She
would finish her education and someday find a wonderful
doctor to share her life and ambitions with. She would
remember this experience with fondness, but she had to
try all the roads of life before she settled on one, go through
lots of experiences and have many loves. She wasn't leaving
just for Ted's sake, but her own as well.

Yet her heart ached. She'd had kisses that came near to
blowing her apart at the seams. She'd had lovemaking that
rivaled the Fourth of July. She'd had the love of a man
who was willing to do anything at all to make her happy.
And she'd found happiness—real, true happiness and a
wonderful family that had accepted her unquestioningly
as one of their own from the very beginning. *Abuelita* was
right. She should not doubt her heart.

Cassie didn't sleep and the ache in her heart didn't go
away.

She heard the clock strike four times and she heard a
door creak somewhere down the hall. Soft footsteps on
the carpet stopped at her door, but only for a few minutes,
then went on down the stairs. The familiar squeak of the
back door was barely audible but she heard it.

She jumped out of bed, drew the drapes and the sliding
glass doors open and stepped out on the balcony. She
could see him walking down the back lane toward the
property he was building on. He carried what looked like
a pillow and a sleeping bag and his head was down as if
he carried the weight of the world on his shoulders.

Evidently he couldn't sleep either. He must be dreading

the good-byes as much as she was. She watched him until he was just a speck in the distance, and wished she walked beside him, if only for one more time and for a couple of hours before she left.

The clock struck five and she was still sitting on the balcony, curled up with her bare feet under her. It was time to put her jeans on so she could help Maria one more time with breakfast. Then she remembered Maria said they wouldn't have breakfast or church this morning. The family planned to sleep late and eat a late brunch. Ted wouldn't be at breakfast anyway. He hadn't returned from the trip down the lane.

Cassie put on jeans, a bra and a shirt, slipped on her sneakers, and went downstairs to find a cup of coffee.

There was a note propped on the coffeepot.

*Goodbye is to painful. So I'll just say, I love you. Ted.*

Her tears flowed down her cheeks and onto her shirt. She grabbed a paper towel and blew her nose. Then she slammed the paper towel down into the wastebasket, and it hit the bottom with a depressingly soggy sound.

She put Ted's note in her hip pocket and walked out the back door with determination. It was the longest mile she ever walked. But Cassie had made up her mind at last. If Ted Wellman hadn't changed his mind in the past few hours, she was going to tell him she loved him and wanted to stay with him forever.

Cassie turned down the lane and was surprised to see a finished cabin sitting where the shell had been only a few weeks before.

But Ted wasn't on the front porch. He had to be somewhere in the house . . . probably snuggled down in a sleeping bag with his handsome face buried in a pillow.

Ted was on the back porch watching the sunrise and didn't see her walking down the lane. He was remembering the day he looked across the bus station diner at a scared little redhead and the way she'd waved at him. Then the whirlwind of life with Cassie had begun. Now all would be peaceful once more. He hated that idea. No, he planned to get up off this porch at eight o'clock and get in his pickup truck, drive to her little town in northern Texas and beg her once again to come home. She might and she might not . . . but, oh, the beauty their lives could know if she would only trust him and her own heart.

Cassie went around the house to the back door and found him staring off into space with a blank look in his eyes. She leaned down before he even realized she was there, kissed him on the cheek.

He looked deep into her green eyes and she, into his brown ones. Words weren't necessary. Cassie was here beside him and the message was clear.

"I love you and I want to stay and be your wife," she said, all in a rush. "Okay?"

"I love you, Cassie." Ted drew her into his arms and kissed her silly. She pulled back, but only to draw a breath.

"What now?" he asked.

"Kiss some more and see where it leads?" she suggested brazenly.

"I mean about us," he said. "I love you. Do you want a real wedding? How long do you really want to be engaged?"

"I had a real wedding. Maybe not a traditional wedding but a wedding nonetheless. You vowed to love me for richer, for poorer, in sickness and in health, and we've consummated the marriage more than once. I expect were as married as we need to be."

"But—" he started.

"Shhh." She touched his lips with her fingertips. "I've had the wedding. What I want now is a honeymoon. No long-legged nurses trying to make off with my husband. No family to come charging up the stairs just when we've jerked our clothes back on. No alarm clock to remind me to get up before Maria gets up to cook breakfast. No one but me and you. My bags are packed. When can we leave?"

"Name the place." He grinned.

"Here and now." She looked up at the two-storey, unfinished house.

"There's no furniture yet. But you can pick out anything and we'll have it delivered today. My bags are packed too. I was leaving at eight o'clock to come to Texas and get you . . . even if I had to rope you again and bring you back over my shoulder," he said. "But we don't have to go anywhere. If you want to stay here—that's fine with me."

"Just a minute," Cassie pulled out of his arms. "Walk halfway up the lane and then turn around and come back to the cabin."

"Why?" he asked.

"Just do it." She pushed him away.

What was she up to now? But he'd do anything to please her and walking up the lane and back didn't seem like much.

She went with him to the front porch, put her arms around his neck and kissed him, then pushed him away. He walked several yards before she called out to him. When he turned, she said, "I love you, darlin'. Have a nice day. The children and I will see you at lunch time."

He ran back to the porch, picked her up and carried her across the threshold into their new home. "We're home, Mrs. Wellman," he said. "And I love you. And all our wonderful, well-behaved imaginary children, too."

"Give me time. We'll get around to having kids eventually," Cassie said, laughing.

"I've got time." Ted dug into the pocket of his jeans and brought out a velvet box. "In fact, I've got a lifetime. I think we've found the answer to all our questions, Cassie."

He opened the box and handed it to her. A brilliant diamond solitaire caught the first rays of the morning sunlight, and made tiny rainbows shine and shimmer around them.

"Love. That's all it takes. That's the only answer."

Cassie looked up at him with tears in her eyes, and watched him slip the ring on the third finger of her left hand.

"You know something, Ted? For once, I'm not going to argue."

And she kissed him, once and for all.